W9-BQT-398

MYTH O MANIA

X

UNDERWORLD LIBRARY
ANCIENT GREECE

AUTHOR
Kate McMullan

TITLE
Get Lost, Odysseus!

DATE DUE	BORROWER'S NAME	
XXVII	*Lord Hades*	
XXXI	*Lord Hades*	

Myth-O-Mania is published by Stone Arch Books
A Capstone Imprint
1710 Roe Crest Drive
North Mankato, Minnesota 56003
www.capstonepub.com

*Library of Congress Cataloging-in-Publication Data is available on the
Library of Congress website.*

Library Binding: 978-1-4342-6016-1 · Paper-Over-Board: 978-1-4342-9194-3 ·
Paperback: 978-1-4342-9193-6 · ebook: 978-1-4965-0078-6
· ebook: 978-1-4965-0041-0

Summary: Hades sets the record straight on the true story of Odysseus.

Cover Illustration: Kevin Keele
Cover, Map, and Interior Design: Kristi Carlson
Production Specialist: Gene Bentdahl

Image Credits: Shutterstock: B. McQueen, Cre8tive Images, Natalia Barsukova,
NY-P, osov, Pablo H. Caridad, Perov Stanislav, Petrov Stanislav Eduardovich,
Selena. Author photo: Phill Lehans

Printed in China by Nordica
0414/CA21400602
032014   008095NORDF14

MYTH-O-MANIA
X

GET LOST, ODYSSEUS

BY
KATE McMULLAN

For my four favorite goddesses:
Erin Owen, Mary Margaret Knolle, Kathryn Knolle, and Marie Knolle

STONE ARCH BOOKS
a capstone imprint

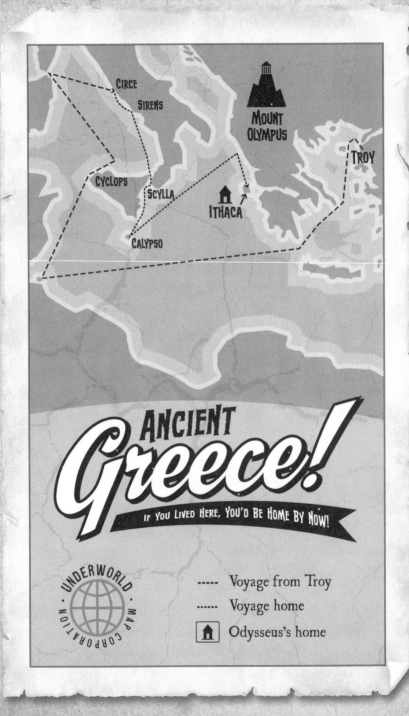

CIRCE
SIRENS
MOUNT OLYMPUS
TROY
CYCLOPS
SCYLLA
ITHACA
CALYPSO

ANCIENT Greece!

IF YOU LIVED HERE, YOU'D BE HOME BY NOW!

UNDERWORLD · MAP CORPORATION ·

----- Voyage from Troy
······ Voyage home
Odysseus's home

TABLE OF CONTENTS

PROLOGUE

Greetings, mortal readers. It's me, King Hades, Lord of the Underworld, back again to tell you the real, true story of a Greek myth. This time it's *The Odyssey*, which is what you mortals call the story of Odysseus's long, torturous trip home from the Trojan War.

Once again, I have to ask: Do you *really* think you know this myth?

Of course you don't.

And why is that?

Right. Because Zeus has meddled with it — big time!

Zeus may be the Ruler of the Universe and the Supreme Thunder God, but he's also a huge myth-o-maniac. (That's old Greek-speak for BIG FAT LIAR!) That god wouldn't know the truth if it hit him on the head. He wouldn't know the truth if he tripped over it. He wouldn't know the truth if it snuck up behind him and bit him on the . . . well, you get the picture. Just take a look at what he and his rewrite nymphs had to say about Odysseus:

Odysseus was a great hero in the Trojan War. When he left Troy to sail home to Ithaca, he was lost at sea for ten years. He begged the brave and mighty Zeus for help, and kindly Zeus sent winds to take him home.

Kindly Zeus? Give me a break. Here's how kindly Zeus helped Odysseus. He sent a terrible thunderstorm that raged on and on for a month. The storm stranded Odysseus and his crew on an island with nothing to eat. And when the storm finally ended and Odysseus and his men were able to sail away, what did kindly Zeus do? He zapped that ship with a thunderbolt — *CRAAAACK!* The ship split in two, the mast fell off, and there was Odysseus, treading water all alone in the middle of the stormy sea. Yep, that's good old kindly Zeus for you.

The day after the Trojan War ended, I went to the beach outside of Troy. The Greeks had reduced that city to a smoldering heap of rubble, and now they were heading home. Odysseus stood at the water's edge, shouting orders to the captains of the twelve black ships that had sailed to Troy with him from the Greek island of Ithaca.

I was standing close enough to Odysseus so that I could see the jagged white scar on his thigh where, long ago, a wild boar had gored him. Ouch! That scar was a doozie.

I could see Odysseus, but he couldn't see me because I was wearing my Helmet of Darkness. When I put on my Helmet — *POOF!* — it makes me and whatever I'm holding invisible. Mortals can't see me and neither can immortals. Nope! I'm the only god in the universe who can roam around unseen by other gods and goddesses. Let me tell you, that Helmet comes in handy.

I watched Odysseus stride up the gangplank of a large black ship. Pretty soon, his ship sailed out of the Trojan harbor, followed by eleven smaller black ships, all bound for Ithaca. The Greeks were skilled sailors, so I figured Odysseus and his men would be home in a few weeks.

Boy, was I ever wrong!

Some immortals can see into the future, but sadly, I'm not one of them. So at the time, I didn't know that Odysseus was going to do something that made my brother Poseidon, god of the seas, angrier than he'd ever been in his whole immortal life. And I didn't have a clue that my bro Po was going to make Odysseus's trip home from the Trojan War a ten-year-long nightmare.

I don't like to interfere in the lives of mortals, but if I'd known what was going to happen, I would have helped Odysseus. Here's why: as the Trojan War raged on and on for ten long years, thousands upon thousands of Greek and Trojan warriors lost their lives and their ghosts came down to dwell in my kingdom. You can't imagine how many ghosts there were! There wasn't room for them all, and the Underworld turned into a great big howling overcrowded mess. I ended up spending all my godly time trying to figure out where to stash a multitude of ghosts. What a headache!

And then clever Odysseus came up with a plan to end the war. Who thinks of hiding a dozen fully armed warriors inside of a huge, hollowed-out wooden horse? Odysseus, that's who. The night the Trojans took that giant warrior-loaded horse into the city of Troy, the war was over and warrior ghosts stopped showing up in the Underworld. Sweet relief! So I was grateful to Odysseus.

Over the years, I've been friends with lots of mortals — wrestling fans like me, mostly. When I go to Wrestle Dome up on earth, we cheer for our favorites together.

But Odysseus wasn't like those other mortals. A minor goddess once offered him immortality.

What mortal wouldn't jump at the chance to live forever? But Odysseus turned the offer down flat. He was one of a kind. Even Zeus had a grudging admiration for the man.

Odysseus wasn't tall, but he was muscle-bound and incredibly strong. Sometimes other mortals mistook him for a god, and did he ever love that!

To tell you the truth, Odysseus was like a god in many ways. He was arrogant, for starters — bragged about everything. He thought he was the biggest deal since hummus met pita. And he could never resist taking credit for his clever plans.

That big ego of his got him into some BIG trouble. I don't know if there's an old Greek-speak word for "jerk," but Odysseus? He could be one.

He was a myth-o-maniac, too, just like Zeus. Liar, liar, toga on fire! Odysseus lied to his crew, he lied to his wife, he lied to his ancient father. He lied to Athena, too, but of course the goddess saw right through him.

Odysseus was also as fearless as a god. When it came to fighting, that man would grab a spear and rush into battle without batting an eye. Or if he saw a place he was curious about, he never stopped to think, *Hold it! I'm mortal. I could DIE in there!* He just jumped right in — and sometimes wished he hadn't, like the time he led his men deep into the Cyclops's cave.

Odysseus could drive me crazy with his arrogance and his bragging and his lies, but there was something about the guy that I couldn't help but like. He was my buddy, and that was that.

Shall I tell you the story of Odysseus's perilous journey home from the Trojan War? How he outwitted a one-eyed giant? How he barely escaped from a cannibal island? How he dodged deadly sea monsters? How he escaped one sorceress only to be taken prisoner by another? How he listened to the Sirens' song and lived to tell the tale?

Mortal reader, are you nodding your head, yes, yes, YES? Are you holding your breath, waiting to hear every word? All right, I'll tell you the story from beginning to end.

Hold on tight.

It's gonna be a wild ride.

Chapter 1
MY BRO PO

It was chilly on the first day of spring that year. I remember because I'd just driven Persephone up to earth so she could do her goddess of spring thing and make everything bloom, from artichokes to zucchinis.

You think moving Persephone is easy? Think again. You should see how many bags, suitcases, and trunks I have to pile into my chariot. Not to mention the sandal boxes.

My steeds, Harley and Davidson, are as mighty as they come. But when I shouted, "Giddy up!" and they started hauling that load, both horses turned their heads around and gave me dirty looks.

It took all day, but we finally got Persephone settled into her little apartment in Athens.

"Thanks, Hades!" she said. "I don't mean to be rude, but I have to get right over to the orchard to see about the fig trees. Not a leaf on any of them yet."

"You go, P-phone," I said, kissing her goodbye. "I'll stop by Spiro's for a cup of java and then head home. Good luck with the figs!"

So there I was, sitting in the immortals' section outside Spiro's, looking at the ships in the harbor and peacefully sipping my coffee, when a voice boomed, "Hades, you old dog!"

I caught a big whiff of Sea Breeze cologne as my brother Poseidon came striding toward me, his mane of blue hair streaming out behind him.

"I ran into Persephone over at the orchard," Po said. "She told me I'd find you here."

Thanks a heap, Persephone, I thought.

My bro Po and I have the same mom and dad. We grew up in the same dark, damp, overcrowded cave of our dad's belly. But right from the get-go, we were different. I like peace and quiet. Po's the original party god, always arranging picnics at some temple. Or planning a late-night rendezvous with a bunch of minor sea goddesses. He couldn't sit still if his immortal life depended on it.

"You gotta see my new sea chariot, Hades," Po went on. "It's twenty-four seahorse power. That baby can MOVE!"

One more thing — Po *loves* speed.

"Great," I said, glancing back at the ships, hoping he'd take the hint and leave.

"You and me are going for a ride, bro!" Po grabbed me by the elbow, toppling my coffee and spilling it all over me. "Oops!" he said. "Good thing you're wearing red, Hades. Me, with my whites? A coffee spill's a disaster. Anyhoo, let's get going. Here's the part you'll love — this chariot goes so fast there's no wave action. Even you won't get seasick!"

"Wish I could go, bro," I said, mopping up the spill, "but I'm having a problem with Cerberus.

If I go away for more than a day, that dog wants nothing to do with me when I get home. It's like he's punishing me or something, so I really need to get back —"

"The mutt can wait!" Po yanked my elbow again. "I'm docked at the end of the pier. Let's roll!"

I tossed down a few coins to pay for my coffee, and we took off.

Fifty yards away, I spotted Po's chariot, a low, sleek craft with a pointed bow and white-capped waves painted on the sides. Tethered to the chariot was a team of giant seahorses — a couple dozen of them! Seahorses are usually timid creatures, but Po's wild-eyed bunch snorted and nipped at each other as they pulled at their halters, raring to go.

"Hop in, Hades!" Po half shoved me into the chariot. The next thing I knew, we were zooming over the water.

Po was right. I wasn't seasick — I was terrified! I was *drosis*ing up a storm. (Drosis? That's old Greek-speak for 'god sweat.')

Salt spray slapped my face, and the speed-crazed seahorses shrieked like demons as they pulled us over the waves.

"It doesn't get any better than this, right, Hades?" Po yelled over the noise.

I managed a nod. Then I shut my godly eyes and didn't open them again until I felt the chariot slow down.

With a final chorus of shrieks, the seahorses came to a stop just off the shore of a rocky little island.

"Seahorses beat dolphins any day of the week!" cried Po.

I leaped out of the chariot. Dry land had never felt so good! I looked around. A little grove of palm trees stood at the center of the island, and a pack of seals lay snoozing beside the rocks.

"Where are we, Po?" I asked.

Po shrugged as he waded into the surf and released his seahorses. "No clue," he said. "I can't keep track of every little island that pokes up out of my seas."

Po had just started dragging his chariot up

onto the beach when suddenly he froze. He stood there, staring into space.

I knew that stare. It meant, *I'm getting a message!* Gods get messages all the time. They're mostly from mortals who are making smoky sacrifices and calling out to a god, begging for something.

Mortals don't generally call out to me, Hades. What are they going to beg me for, a room with a view at Motel Styx? But I could tell from the dazed look on Po's face that he was receiving one very serious message.

For a god with a short attention span, Po listened for quite a while. His face grew red, then redder. His sea-blue eyes began to flash with anger.

Finally, he shook his head and blinked. He looked sort of seasick himself.

"What's wrong, Po?" I asked.

"Odysseus has blinded my son!" he wailed.

"No! That's awful!" I said. "Uh . . . which one?" Poseidon had dozens of sons, and not one of them was what you'd call a nice guy.

"Polyphemus!" shouted Po.

"What?" I cried. "That's impossible. Polyphemus is a Cyclops. A giant! A mere mortal like Odysseus couldn't hurt him."

Po paced up and down the beach, wild-eyed. "My son wants revenge!" he said. "Polyphemus begged me to punish Odysseus for his vile deed. He wants Odysseus to get lost on his trip home and have the most terrible voyage ever."

"Uh-oh," I muttered. As ruler of the seas, Po could make that happen.

"And if Odysseus makes it back home to Ithaca?" Po ranted on. "Polyphemus begged me to make sure that he finds *worse* trouble waiting for him there!"

"Calm down, Po," I said. "There must be some mistake."

But Po wasn't even close to calming down.

"I'll send hurricane-force winds to blow his ships onto the rocks!" he roared. "I'll send giant waves to swamp his ships and sink them to the bottom of the sea! That mortal will wish he'd never laid eyes on my son."

With that, Po plunged back into the sea and hitched up his seahorses again. He jumped into his sea chariot.

"I know you and Odysseus are big buddies!" Po yelled at me over his squealing team. "But if you help that wily mortal, Hades, I'll find out about it. I will! And I'll make your life as miserable as I'm about to make his!"

"Don't start with me, Po!" I yelled back to him.

"There will be flooding in the Underworld!" Po howled. "Tidal waves! Tsunamis!"

My heart sank. Po wasn't kidding. He was ready to destroy my kingdom!

"You won't believe the damage I can do with water!" Po shouted. "Thick black mold will ooze from your palace walls! You'll never get rid of it."

"You wouldn't!" I cried.

"I will!" shouted Po. "Unless you swear to me that you will not help Odysseus."

"Take it easy, bro —"

"No!" He cut me off. "Swear! Or you'll be so sorry."

"All right, I swear!" I shouted. "I won't help Odysseus."

"Swear it on the River Styx!" shrieked Po.

I swallowed. An oath sworn on the River Styx could never be broken. But what choice did I have? I couldn't let him wreck Villa Pluto and the Underworld. I couldn't let him destroy Odysseus, either. That mortal couldn't have harmed Polyphemus, I was sure of it.

I glared at Po. "I, King Hades," I said from between my gritted teeth, "firstborn of the gods; son of Cronus and Rhea; Ruler of the Underworld; god of wealth; husband of Persephone, goddess of spring; master of Cerberus, Guard Dog of the Gates of the Underworld; wrestling aficionado; pizza eater —"

"Get on with it!" cried Po.

". . . do solemnly swear on the River Styx not to help Odysseus directly," I added really fast.

Po nodded. He seemed satisfied. He yanked the seahorse reins, turned his team around, and zoomed off over the waves.

I watched him go, my hot-tempered younger

brother. Yes, he'd forced me to swear on the River Styx. But buried in my longer-than-necessary oath was a one-word escape hatch.

Directly.

I smiled. Short of helping Odysseus myself, I was determined to do everything within my godly power to make sure that mortal made it safely home. No way was I going to let my blue-haired little brother get the best of me. No way!

CHAPTER II
THE CYCLOPS

As soon as Po was out of sight, I reached into my robe pocket and pulled out my wallet. Persephone had given it to me, and she'd had it monogrammed with gold letters that spelled out K.H.R.O.T.U., for King Hades, Ruler of the Underworld.

It looks like any ordinary wallet, but looks can be deceiving. I can open that baby up, toss in whatever I want— a few Bacon Bits for Cerbie or a spare chariot wheel — and the wallet expands to hold it all. But when I close it? That wallet shrinks back down to pocket size.

Three things I always carry in my K.H.R.O.T.U. wallet are:

- *an extra robe*
- *my Helmet of Darkness*
- *a shaker of ambro-salt*

In case you're wondering about that last item, it's a condensed form of ambrosia, the food of the gods. If we immortals don't have ambrosia or nectar, the drink of the gods, we won't die — we can't, really — but we shrivel up and start looking like wrinkly old prunes. Wrinkly prune is not a good look for me, which is why I make sure I always have my ambro-salt handy. A few sprinkles turn mortal food into an ambrosia-laced treat.

I dug my Helmet out of my wallet and put it on.

POOF!

I was invisible and ready to search for Odysseus.

Like all major deities, I can astro-travel wherever I want to go. I chant a *ZIP* code, and *ZZZZZZZIP!* I'm there.

But *ZIPPING* around from island to island in the Greek seas wasn't easy. I didn't know the names of most of the islands, much less their *ZIP* codes. So it took me a while, but at last I landed on Aeolia, an island I knew. It belonged to Aeolus, King of the Winds. And there in the harbor I spied twelve black ships.

Bingo!

I scouted out the place, and found Odysseus sitting by himself on a hilltop above the king's palace, looking down at the sea.

I strode over to him and took off my Helmet.

FOOP!

If the God of the Underworld suddenly appeared out of nowhere, most mortals would jump out of their skins. But Odysseus? All he did was look up at me and smile.

"Hey, Hades!" he said. "What's all over your robe?"

I glanced down. "Oh, uh . . . coffee." Po had been wrong about the stain not showing up on red.

I sat down on the hill beside Odysseus. "So,"

I said, "I hear you had a little run-in with a Cyclops."

Odysseus grinned. "Word travels fast."

"Tell me what happened," I said.

"Okay," said Odysseus. "You won't believe how I got myself and my men — well, most of them anyway — out of the Cyclops's cave."

"Try me," I said.

"A storm blew my twelve black ships into a bay beside a rugged, hilly island," he began. "We dropped anchor, hoping to find people on it who'd be kind to wanderers, as Zeus decrees."

Who knows why, but Zeus loved to knock on people's doors disguised as a mortal beggar or a peddler. To make sure he'd be well-treated, he had decreed that mortals had to welcome every stranger who showed up at their door. They weren't allowed to ask the stranger any questions — not even his name — until they'd brought him into their home, provided him with a fine meal and plenty of good wine, and offered the stranger a place to sleep. And they had to give the stranger a pricey host gift, too.

How like Zeus to figure out a way to mooch off mortals!

"The next day, " Odysseus went on, "I chose twelve men, and we rowed over to the island in a small boat. We hiked up a steep hill, bringing along a big jar of strong wine to share with whomever we might meet. Before long, we came to the entrance of a cave. Lots of empty sheep pens stood around it, so we figured a shepherd lived there and that he was out, tending his flock. I was curious to see what his cave looked like, so I led my men inside, where we found great baskets of cheese and buckets of sheep's milk. We helped ourselves, and when our bellies were full, we settled down deep within the cave to wait for our host."

"That seems like a risky thing to do," I said.

"Turns out it was," Odysseus admitted. "After a while we heard bleating. Soon dozens of sheep trotted into the cave. They were real beauties, Hades. And huge! Three times the size of any sheep I'd ever seen, and they were covered in clouds of thick white fleece. Behind them came their shepherd," he continued. "He was a monster! A giant with one huge, round eye in the center of his forehead!"

"A Cyclops," I said.

Odysseus nodded. "The Cyclops rolled an enormous boulder into the mouth of the cave, blocking it," he went on. "Then he built a fire, and in the firelight, he spied me and my twelve men. I quickly spoke up, saying that we were Greeks. That we'd fought a war, that we'd gotten lost sailing back to our home in Ithaca, and that a storm had tossed our ship onto his island. I thanked the Cyclops for the food we'd eaten, and said that since Zeus demanded that hosts feed weary strangers, we figured eating it was okay. I thought we were getting along just fine, Hades, but you know what he said?"

"More or less," I muttered.

"He said he cared nothing for the words of Zeus. That he cared only for the words of his father, Poseidon. And then he . . . he . . ." Odysseus looked a little green. "He grabbed two of my men and ate them! Chewed them up and swallowed them and washed them down with goat's milk." Odysseus hung his head, remembering the awful moment.

"Poseidon's offspring are a bad bunch," I said.

Odysseus sighed. "At last the Cyclops went to sleep beside the fire," he continued. "I crept close to the monster. I drew my sword and was about to slice his throat when it hit me — if I killed him, my men and I would be trapped inside the cave, for the boulder that sealed the entrance was far too big for us to move."

"Good thinking," I said.

"The next morning, the Cyclops woke up and ate two more of my men." Odysseus shuddered. "He milked his fleecy sheep, then shoved the boulder away from the mouth of the cave. He drove his sheep out and then rolled the huge stone back in place, keeping us trapped inside."

"You must have thought you were doomed," I said.

"You know me, Hades," said Odysseus. "I never think that. Instead, I came up with a clever plan."

"A little late for four of your men," I muttered. "But go on."

"The Cyclops had a wooden walking stick leaning against the cave wall," Odysseus said. "It was as thick as a tree trunk. When the Cyclops left us alone in the cave that morning, my men and I took our swords and whittled the walking stick to a sharp point. Then we hid it at the back of the cave.

"At end of day, the Cyclops and his sheep returned," he continued. "As before, the monster blocked the mouth of the cave with the boulder and made a fire. And then he . . . he . . ."

"Ate two more of your men," I finished for him.

The poor mortal nodded. "I poured some of the wine I'd brought into one of the Cyclops's bowls, mixed it with water, and took it to him, saying it would be a fine thing for washing down his . . . his . . . dinner."

Odysseus looked sick to his stomach. "Our monstrous host gulped down the wine and shouted for more. I gave him more. And more!

After he'd drunk three bowls full, he said he wanted to give me a host gift and he asked my name."

"Did you tell him?" I asked.

"I told him my name was Nobody." Odysseus looked very pleased with himself. "Then the Cyclops told me what my gift was — I'd be eaten last of all."

"Not your usual host gift," I said.

"After another bowl of wine," Odysseus went on, "the Cyclops fell into a deep sleep. His snores rumbled like thunder. My six remaining men and I fetched the walking stick. We held the pointed end in the coals of the fire until it glowed red-hot. Then we approached the sleeping giant. Together we raised the red-hot walking stick and jammed it into the Cyclops's eye!"

I tried not to think what THAT must have felt like.

"A huge cloud of red steam rose from the bloody eyeball, hissing like a thousand snakes." Odysseus grinned. "The Cyclops howled in pain."

I was turning green just listening to this tale.

But it told me that Po'd had it right. Odysseus had blinded his giant son.

"The Cyclops jumped up, yelling and shouting, and yanked the stick from his eye," Odysseus went on. "Footsteps sounded from outside the cave. A deep voice shouted, 'Polyphemus! Our brother! Why are you yelling?'

"And Polyphemus shouted back, 'Nobody has hurt me!'

"'Well, if nobody has hurt you,' called his brother, 'then you don't need our help.' And the other Cyclopes went away." Odysseus smiled proudly.

"Very clever, Odysseus," I said. "But how did you get out of the cave?"

"That was the cleverest part!" cried Odysseus. "In the night, by the glow of embers from the fire, I took lengths of rope I'd found inside the cave and I bound the sheep together in groups of three. Then I tied one of my men under the belly of each middle sheep.

"When morning came, Polyphemus shoved the boulder away from the mouth of the cave, as usual," Odysseus went on. "Even though he could no longer see, he was not about to let us men escape. So, as I suspected he might, he sat in the mouth of the cave and felt the backs of the big, fleecy sheep as they crowded past him on their way outside. He never thought to feel under the bellies of those sheep, where my men were hidden.

"When all my men were safely out of the cave, I swung myself underneath the biggest sheep and held tight to its fleece," Odysseus said. "The sheep ran out of the cave and I was free. I dropped to the ground, cut my men loose, and we ran for our ship, driving the sheep along with us.

"Polyphemus heard the sheep bleating, and he stumbled out of his cave," he added. "The Cyclops staggered blindly down the hill after us, but we ran faster. We made it to our boat, carried the sheep aboard, and quickly rowed away. When we were some distance from the island, I shouted, loud and clear, 'Listen up, Polyphemus, you great big hairy lug of a bully! Hear me, you sheep-stinking, cheese-eating, knuckle-dragging monster! It was I who blinded you. I, Odysseus!'"

My heart sank. If only he hadn't done that! Then Polyphemus would have had no way of knowing who had blinded him. And he couldn't have begged his father to wreak a horrible revenge on Odysseus. But Odysseus always had to take credit for his clever schemes, and this time was no exception.

"The Cyclops picked up a huge boulder," Odysseus went on. "He shouted, 'GET LOST, ODYSSEUS!' And he flung the boulder in the direction of my voice. It splashed into the water, barely missing us. Our boat rocked like crazy, but we rowed on and made it to the twelve black ships."

"You were lucky," I offered.

"We were," agreed Odysseus. "As we sailed away, we heard the Cyclops calling out to his father, Poseidon, saying how I'd blinded him. He begged Poseidon to make sure I got lost on my way home. And that when I did come home —"

"You should find *worse* trouble waiting for you there," I finished for him.

"How'd you know that, Hades?" asked Odysseus.

"We gods know things." I shook my head. "You're trying to sail home, and now you've made an enemy of the god of the seas. That is not a clever plan, Odysseus."

"What's done is done." Odysseus shrugged. "Anyway, you know Aeolus, King of the Winds?"

"Not well," I said. "But I know that the winds obey his commands."

"That's right," said Odysseus. "And the king says he's going to send the West Wind to speed us home to Ithaca."

"What if other winds blow you off course?" I asked.

"They can't," said Odysseus.

"And why is that?" I asked.

"Because King Aeolus is giving me a super host gift," said Odysseus. "I'm supposed to keep it secret, because the king doesn't want every wanderer who lands on his island asking for this gift, but I'll tell you, Hades. It's an ox-hide bag with all the other winds in the world trapped inside it."

He smiled and waggled his eyebrows. How he reminded me of my cocky little brother Zeus! Always so sure of himself. Never thinking ahead or doubting for a moment that maybe, just maybe, something could go terribly wrong.

"Once we're on dry land in Ithaca," Odysseus continued, "I'll open the bag and let the winds out. But the trip home? That's gonna be easy-peasy, Hades. Piece of baklava!"

Chapter III
GIANT CANNIBALS

After our little talk, I left Odysseus on King Aeolus's island and went back home to the Underworld.

Cerberus had always had a sense of when I was coming home, and he'd wait on the bank of the River Styx to greet me. He'd hop into my chariot, and we'd drive back to the palace together. But this time when I arrived home, that dog was nowhere to be seen, so I had to drive home solo.

"Cerbie!" I called as I walked into my palace. "Cerbie, I'm home!"

But no three-headed Guard Dog of the Underworld came running.

"Cerberus? Where are you, boy, boy, boy?" I called.

As I headed for my den, my first lieutenant, Hypnos, the god of sleep, came rushing down the hallway toward me.

"Oh, Lord Hades, am I ever glad to see you!" he cried.

I frowned. "You look terrible, Hypnos," I said. "What's wrong?"

"I haven't slept a wink for three weeks!" Hypnos said. "Not since you left to drive Queen Persephone up to earth."

"But why?" I asked.

"It's Cerberus," said Hypnos. "That dog won't stop howling!"

"Well, you can't blame a dog for missing his master," I said as Hypnos began walking along at my side. "Did you give him the Liver Yum-Dingers I got for him?"

"He spit them out," Hypnos said. "All three of them."

Those dog treats had cost me a fortune. "What about the Squeaky Squirrel chewy toys?" I asked.

"He wouldn't even look at them," said Hypnos.

I sighed. "Cerbie, come!" I called. Not for the first time, I wished I'd taken him to obedience school when he was a little triple-headed pup.

Hypnos and I looked high and low around the palace for that dog. Finally I found him curled up under my throne.

I got down on my godly hands and knees. "Cerbie! Daddy's home!" I said.

Each head opened one eye and closed it again.

So much for my greeting.

That dog didn't come near me for three whole days. Finally, one night, as I opened a box of piping hot pepperoni pizza, Cerbie trotted into the den. I gave all his heads a pat, and his tummy, too, and after a triple helping of pizza, he seemed to forgive me for going off and leaving him.

But why the sudden change in Cerbie's behavior? Was something seriously wrong with my pooch? I couldn't figure it out.

Cerbie wasn't my only worry. I couldn't get my mind off Odysseus. He didn't seem at all bothered by the fact that he'd angered the god of the seas. I figured I'd better check on him, and I went to get dressed. When Cerbie saw me in my road robe, that dog threw his heads back and gave an ichor-chilling triple howl.

"I'll be back, Cerbie," I yelled over the noise. "I have to go make sure Odysseus is okay," I added, as if he could understand me. And maybe he could. Who knew?

I drove my chariot to the water taxi, and the whole way there, I could hear Cerberus yowling.

* * *

Once I was out of my kingdom, I *ZIPPED* to a hilltop on King Aeolus's island. From there I caught sight of Odysseus's men loading the twelve Greek ships.

42

A couple of King Aeolus's servants were stowing what looked like a giant balloon under the bow of Odysseus's ship. Had to be the bag that held all the winds.

Before long, the black ships sailed out of the harbor, heading for Ithaca. A steady West Wind filled their sails, just as Odysseus had said it would. At the rate they were going, I figured it would take them about ten days to get home.

I planned to check on them every day, and hang out for a while just above the ships in Hover Mode.

When we gods are astro-traveling, Hover Mode is like hitting pause. It allows us to suspend ourselves midair and observe what's going on down below.

But I couldn't hover 24/7, so I surprised Persephone by showing up at her little apartment in Athens. The two of us went out to dinner every night, and then sometimes I caught a match at Wrestle Dome. But every day, when Persephone went off to do her blooming work, I *ZZZZZZIPPED* around to see how things were going with the Greek ships.

And every day, I saw Odysseus standing at the helm of the lead ship, steering. It seemed as if he didn't trust anyone but himself to get his fleet back home.

The West Wind kept blowing steadily, and each day the black ships sailed closer to Ithaca. I began to think that my bro Po had forgotten all about wreaking havoc on Odysseus.

On the tenth day, a crewman called, "Land ho! Ithaca!"

I wanted to be there for Odysseus's homecoming, so I *ZIPPED* invisibly onto the lead ship. To my surprise, I found Odysseus stretched out in the stern, sound asleep. The poor mortal had been steering for ten days and nights. He had to be exhausted. But still, he was so close to home. Why would he take a nap now?

Just then, one of the other Greek ships pulled close to Odysseus's craft.

A crewman from that ship glanced at the sleeping captain. Then, keeping his voice low, he said, "We've heard whispers of treasure hidden in that ox-hide bag."

"Whispers that Odysseus plans to keep the treasure for himself alone," a second crewman added.

"Odysseus has never told us what's inside the bag," one of Odysseus's crewmen said. Now he, too, eyed his captain suspiciously.

Whispers? Treasures? What was going on? The hairs on the back of my godly neck began to prickle, which often happens when I sense disaster looming.

I couldn't wake Odysseus myself, as I'd sworn not to help him directly.

Instead, I elbowed one of the crew members so that he lost his balance and tripped over the sleeping hero.

But it didn't work. Odysseus slept on.

I watched helplessly as other black vessels pulled even with Odysseus's ship. Men hopped aboard. They yanked the bag of winds out from under the bow and cut the ropes that held it shut.

The bag opened, and a terrible roar filled the air! Storm winds howled! Huge waves rocked the Greek ships!

Odysseus woke with a start. His ships were tilting and spinning as storm winds raged. The wild East Wind was blowing them away from Ithaca and back toward Aeolia at a terrific speed.

There was no way for me to help Odysseus now. And given that I can get seasick in a wading pool, there was no way I was sticking with him on a bucking ship.

ZZZZZZZZZZZIP!

I landed invisibly on a hill above King Aeolus's harbor, for I feared that the winds would blow them back to where they'd started. As I waited to catch sight of the Greek ships, I wondered — had Po ordered some of his sea nymphs to whisper of secret treasure to the Greek crewman? Had Po somehow put a sleeping spell on Odysseus?

Before long, I caught sight of the black ships, all twelve of them, helpless in the force of the terrible winds. Once the ships had been blown into the harbor, the winds died down. It was eerie, the way they stopped blowing so suddenly.

An Aeolean guard called out news of the ships. King Aeolus and his people ran down to the harbor.

"Hiya, King," called Odysseus from the lead ship. "Listen, we had a little accident. Any way you could bag up those crazy winds again?"

"I will not!" cried the King of the Winds. "You must be cursed by some god to have lost my precious host gift and be blown back here!"

King Aeolus had that right. Po was really letting the poor mortal have it!

"It would be a crime for me to help one cursed by a god," King Aeolus shouted. "Be gone! Now! Before I send winds to rip your sails to shreds!"

"Okay, okay," said Odysseus. "I get the message. How about sending a little puff of wind to get us out of the harbor?"

"You'll get nothing more from me!" shouted King Aeolus.

Then he and his people turned away from

the harbor and walked back to their city, leaving Odysseus and the twelve Greek ships becalmed in the harbor.

"Get out the oars, guys," said Odysseus. "It's gonna be a long trip home."

At the time, Odysseus didn't have a clue just how long.

* * *

I wanted to get home to Cerberus. The longer I stayed away, the snarkier that dog was going to be when I finally got home.

But I couldn't leave Odysseus. Not yet. So I stuck around Athens with Persephone for a while longer to keep tabs on the mortal hero.

Sadly for Odysseus, King Aeolus had meant what he said. He never sent even a small gust of wind to help the Greeks get home. Odysseus and his crew rowed with all their might, but they didn't make much progress. I thought I'd be back home in a week or two, but I ended up staying on earth for months.

When I wasn't checking on Odysseus, I was

sitting at a table in the Athens Public Library reading scrolls on dog behavior and trying to figure out what was wrong with Cerberus. Check out my reading list:

You CAN Train Your Dog! by Ken I. Reely

Come Inside, Puppy! by Doris Open

Feed Your Dog Right by Norma Cookies

Dog Bites! by Drew Blood

Dogs Don't Like Me by Ivanna Katt

The Worst Pooch in the World by Gladys Knottmydawg

But nothing in those scrolls explained Cerbie's howling when I left home or his hiding and sulking when I came back. To be honest, I was starting to think Cerbie might need a doggie shrink.

The next time I checked on Odysseus, I found the Greek ships anchored in a harbor surrounded by high, steep cliffs. I counted eleven Greek ships. I counted again.

Eleven?

Then I spotted Odysseus's ship. It was tied to a jagged rock at the mouth of the harbor. As I watched, Odysseus and three of his men left the ship. I figured they were going to explore the island, so I tagged invisibly behind.

As the men walked, one of the crewmen said, "Why did we not sail into the harbor with the other ships, Odysseus?"

"I'm still ticked off at those guys for opening the wind bag," Odysseus growled. "If it weren't for those bozos, we'd all be home now."

"Look," said a second crewman. "Here comes a girl."

"A giant girl," said a third.

He wasn't kidding. This girl was almost as tall as a god. She had big brown eyes and straw-colored hair that sprouted from her head like a fountain. I remembered Persephone telling me that this style was called the "pony tail."

"Hello there, strangers!" boomed the giant girl. "Welcome to Laestrygonia!" She smiled, showing a large mouth filled with sharp, pointy teeth. "Come meet my father, King Antiphates. He's about to have his supper."

"We could use some supper ourselves," said Odysseus.

"My father the king loves to have strangers

for supper," the giant girl said, licking her lips in a wolfish way. "Follow me."

The hairs on the back of my godly neck started prickling again. You'd think that after Odysseus's experience with the giant Cyclops, he'd be wary of giants. Even two-eyed giants. You'd think that maybe when a giant girl said, "Follow me," he'd say, "Uh, no thanks," and get out of there.

But we're talking about Odysseus here. Of course, he was only too happy to follow the giant girl and meet her father. He probably wanted to see what sort of a king the man was.

I followed invisibly along as the giant girl led Odysseus and his men up a steep hill. At the top, a huge gray-stone palace sat on the edge of a cliff above the harbor. The giant girl cupped her hands to her mouth. "Father, come out!" she called. "We've got company for supper!"

A moment later, King Antiphates strode out of the palace. He was far taller than his giant daughter, but he had the same brown eyes and straw-colored hair. At the sight of him, the hairs on the back of my neck stood up and prickled like a hundred beestings. Something terrible was about to happen!

The giant king walked straight to Odysseus and his three men. Without a word, he grabbed up one of the crewmen, held him upside down over his giant mouth, and . . .

HOW MUCH DO YOU KNOW ABOUT GIANT KINGS? FIND OUT BY TAKING HADES'S SPECIAL MULTIPLE-CHOICE QUIZ!

A. Did the giant king shake that crewman hoping his lunch money would fall out of his pockets?

B. Did the giant king mistake the crewman for a dentist and open his mouth really wide to show him a rotten tooth?

C. Did the giant king hold that crewman upside down so he could watch his face turn red?

D. Did the giant king drop that crewman into his mouth and swallow him whole?

E. Did the giant king toss the crewman into his mouth and chew him up?

Did you pick D or E? Congratulations! One of them must be right, but I can't tell you which one because I couldn't watch what happened. Poor Odysseus! He and his men had stumbled onto a cannibal island.

"RUN!" Odysseus shouted to the two men still with him. "Warn the others!"

The three turned and raced pell-mell down the hill to their ship.

The king began to howl. As he howled, Laestrygonians came running to the palace carrying wicked-looking spears attached to coils of rope.

"Ships in the harbor!" the king cried. "Go fish!"

I *ZZZZIPPED* to the top of the highest cliff. From there, I could see the eleven black ships. Clearly they'd heard the ruckus. Crewmen were frantically hoisting their sails.

But the giant Laestrygonians picked up huge boulders and hurled them into the harbor. Hundreds of boulders rained down on the ships, smashing them to bits and sinking them.

The poor crewmen jumped overboard to save themselves, but it was no use. The cannibals speared them like so many unlucky fish.

I turned away from the horrors of the harbor just in time to see Odysseus and the two remaining crewmen jump into their ship. Another crewman quickly untied it from the rock.

"ROW!" Odysseus bellowed to his crew. "ROW FOR YOUR LIVES!"

Odysseus's ship sped away from Laestrygonia and out to the open sea, leaving behind the eleven other Greek ships that had sunk to the bottom of the sea, and their poor comrades who'd been harpooned by the cannibals.

Now I understood what the giant girl had meant when she'd said that the king loved *having strangers for supper*!

Po'd had a hand in steering Odysseus to this cannibal island, I was sure of it.

Odysseus had sailed from Troy with twelve black ships and hundreds of men. Now he had one ship and maybe two dozen men. And all because that mortal couldn't resist shouting out his name to claim credit for blinding Po's son, Polyphemus, the Cyclops.

CHAPTER IV

CIRCE THE SORCERESS

I'd been away almost a year, and was itching to get back home. Kingdoms don't run themselves, you know. And when I'm not around, things in the Underworld have a way of going wrong.

Take King di Minos. He'd been king of Crete. That seemed like a big job, so when he showed up in my kingdom, I made him a judge. He ruled over the Underworld Courthouse and decided where each ghost should spend eternity. He's supposed to send the ghosts of the good to peaceful Elysium, the ghosts of the not-so-good to the Asphodel Fields, and ghosts of the wicked to fiery Tartarus. But when I'm not there? Di Minos totally slacks off. If he's in a bad mood, he sends all the ghosts to be fried in Tartarus. If he's feeling jolly, he'll send them all to Elysium. It takes me forever to get it all sorted out.

You'd think my two lieutenants, Hypnos, god of sleep, and his brother, Thanatos, god of death, could carry on for a while when I'm away. But if too many ghosts show up, they get all flustered, and instead of taking action to solve the problem, they take naps.

As you can imagine, when I got back to the Underworld after being away for so long, I had my godly hands full. But dealing with ghostly problems was easy compared to what I was going through with the Guard Dog of the Underworld. For days, Cerberus wouldn't even look at me, not with any of his six big brown eyes.

Did Cerbie feel unloved? I began brushing him twice a day to show I cared. His coat shone, but he still wouldn't make eye contact.

I thought back to one of the scrolls I'd read at the library in Athens: *Feed Your Dog Right* by Norma Cookies. So I cut out the cookies and treats.

The looks Cerbie gave me at his usual treat times weren't pretty. And depriving that dog of his cookies only seemed to make things worse.

Could Cerbie's sudden behavior change be the result of some rare vitamin deficiency? I bought VitaPup Powder and made him Poochie Smoothies.

He turned up his noses.

Had Cerbie developed a food allergy? I tossed out his old kibble and switched that dog to Mighty Meaty Feasty. Three bowls for breakfast and three more for dinner were insanely expensive. I'm god of wealth, so the money wasn't a big deal, but even Mighty Meaty Feasty didn't do the trick. The next time I *ZIPPED* away to see about Odysseus, that dog howled louder than a kennel full of lovesick beagles.

* * *

I *ZZZZIPPED* around the Aegean Sea for a couple of days, searching for Odysseus. I finally found his ship anchored off an island covered with lots of flowering trees and bushes. P-phone had once told me about this flower-filled island, and how it was home to some minor goddess. But which one? I couldn't remember what she'd said.

As I hiked invisibly around the island, looking for our hero, I pulled my phone out of my robe pocket and called Persephone. (Have I mentioned that we gods all have cell phones? Oh, yeah. We invented them long before you mortals came up with the idea.) Her phone rang and rang, but this was a busy time of year for the goddess of spring and she didn't pick up. I didn't bother leaving a message.

At last I came upon Odysseus and a few of his crewmen. They were roasting deer meat over a fire. Where was the rest of the crew? I hoped they hadn't been eaten by some monster!

Unseen, thanks to my Helmet of Darkness, I hung out not far from the campfire to listen in and find out what was going on.

"Shouldn't your cousin Rylo and the others be back by now, Odysseus?" asked a crewman as he turned the meat on a spit.

Just then I heard rustling in the brush. Another crewman burst into camp.

"Woe is us!" he cried. The poor mortal was trembling and close to tears.

Odysseus jumped up. "Rylo!" he shouted. "What's wrong?"

A crewman gave Rylo a drink of water and helped him sit down by the fire.

"Tell us what happened," said Odysseus.

"My twenty-two men and I walked through the woods until we came to a clearing," Rylo said. "In the clearing stood a stone cottage. Tame lions and wolves roamed around it. They were friendly beasts, and licked our hands like dogs."

"Some magic is at work," muttered Odysseus. "Go on."

"Inside the cottage, we heard a woman singing," said Rylo. "One of my men called out to her, and she came to the door. She was tall and wore a fine gold-trimmed robe. She invited us inside."

The poor mortal started shaking again. Something terrible must have happened!

"My men went eagerly into the cottage," Rylo continued. "But I was cautious. I hid behind a tree, waiting to see what might happen."

"A wise move," said Odysseus.

Wiser than you would have been, Odysseus, I thought. That mortal didn't know the meaning of the word "cautious."

"I peered in through the window," Rylo went on. "The woman was mixing what looked like wine and water in a golden bowl. She poured the mixture into cups and gave them to my men, who drank them down. I began to think I had been foolish to stay behind. I was about to enter the cottage myself when I saw the woman hold up a thin wooden wand. She quickly touched my men with the wand, and they all turned into pigs!"

"Pigs?" cried the listening crewmen. "Pigs?"

Pigs. It was all coming back to me now. A

minor goddess who thought it was a hoot to turn men into pigs. What was her name? I couldn't think.

Odysseus frowned. "She must have mixed some potion with the wine," he muttered.

"My poor pig-men squealed horribly as she herded them out of her cottage and into a pigsty," Rylo went on. "As they passed my hiding spot, I could see tears streaming down their piggy cheeks."

Remembering it all, Rylo began to cry. After what he'd seen, who could blame him?

Odysseus leaped to his feet. He stuck his sword into his belt and grabbed his bow. "We must rescue our men!" he cried. "Lead the way, Rylo!"

"I can't go back!" Rylo wailed. "And if you go, you shall end up in the pigpen, too!"

But of course Odysseus didn't listen. He stomped off into the woods, leaving his men behind.

My godly head was spinning. I couldn't help Odysseus, but if I did nothing, Rylo's terrible prediction would come true. Odysseus could spend the rest of his life in a pigpen. Or end up on a platter with an apple in his mouth!

Now I remembered who lived on this island — Circe. She was a powerful sorceress known to have magical potions that tamed wild beasts and turned men into swine.

Was there any way to make her potions harmless, I wondered? Who knew about potions and antidotes?

I racked my brain. At last it came to me: Hermes.

Sure, he was the messenger of the gods. And he drove the ghosts of mortals down to my kingdom. But he was also god of — well, you name it, and Hermes was most likely god of it. And that included medicine. If any god could help Odysseus, it was Hermes.

I dug out my phone, hit the "anonymous call" button so my name wouldn't show up on his caller ID, and punched in his number.

"Hermes here," he answered. "Giant slayer as well as god of travelers, roads, thieves, business, animal husbandry, hospitality, heralds, diplomacy, trade, language, writing — both fiction and nonfiction — stargazing, astrology, medicine, potions, antidotes, persuasion, cunning, athletic events, and gym class. How may I help you?"

Potions? Antidotes? Bingo!

Let me say right up front that I'm not proud of what I was about to do.

"Hermes?" I said in a high, squeaky voice. "You must go to Circe's island, on the double! The mortal Odysseus needs your help!"

"Who is this?" said Hermes.

I kept quiet.

"Has Circe turned Odysseus into a porker?" he asked.

I didn't say.

"All right, all right, I'm going," said Hermes. *Click!*

My heart beat like a drum. I hadn't helped Odysseus. I'd only asked another god to help him. Still, if Po found out what I'd done, he might well turn the Underworld into Mold City!

Seconds later, Hermes landed on the path.

I still had on my Helmet, so he didn't see me watching invisibly as he transformed himself into a young man and caught up with Odysseus, who was walking at a rapid clip.

"Greetings, my friend!" called Hermes in disguise.

"Can't talk now," said Odysseus.

"I know where you're headed in such a hurry," said Hermes. "To the home of Circe the Sorceress, right?"

"That's who lives here?" asked Odysseus.

Hermes nodded. "I'll bet she's changed your comrades into pigs."

"Yes!" cried Odysseus. "And I am going to rescue my men."

"Big mistake!" said Hermes. "She'll just turn you into a piggie, too."

Odysseus stopped.

"Only one thing can protect you." Hermes reached down and pulled up a small, white-flowered plant growing beside the path. "Put this plant inside your robe, next to your heart," he said.

"With all that dirt clinging to the roots?" asked Odysseus.

"Dirt, schmirt," said Hermes. "This is a magical plant. If you keep it over your heart, you can drink Circe's potion and you won't turn into a pig."

"Awright!" Odysseus smashed that plant against his chest, roots, dirt, and all. Then he turned and hurried on to Circe's cottage.

"Good luck!" Hermes called after him. And then *ZZZZIP!* He was gone.

I stuck invisibly with Odysseus as he made his way to Circe. When he reached the clearing, our hero walked boldly toward the stone cottage. He paid no attention to the tawny yellow lions that ran over to him and brushed against his legs like oversized house cats. He ignored the gray wolves as they trotted toward him, wagging their tails. When the pigs in the sty saw him, they began snorting and grunting, but Odysseus looked away from them and called out, "Circe!"

The sorceress came to the door of her cottage. "Come in, weary traveler," she said.

Odysseus strode into the cottage, and I slipped in behind him.

"Sit in my silver chair, traveler, and I'll pour you some wine," said Circe.

Odysseus sat down while Circe mixed wine and water and who knows what else in her golden bowl. She poured the mixture into a cup.

"Here you are," she said, handing the cup to Odysseus. "Drink every drop!"

Odysseus downed the potion in a single gulp.

Now Circe tapped him with her wooden wand. "To the sty with you!" she cried.

"Why would I want to go to a sty?" said Odysseus.

Circe frowned. She tapped him again. And again.

"It's not working, is it?" said Odysseus.

"Who are you to resist my powers?" cried Circe. "Wait. I know. You are Odysseus!"

Odysseus grinned. "So, I'm famous way out here in the boonies, huh?"

"It was foretold that you would stop here on your way home from Troy," said Circe. "And so you have." She smiled. "I shall have my handmaidens make us a fine feast, and we shall talk of many things."

"Not so fast, Circe," said Odysseus. "First, turn my men back into men."

Circe sighed. "Oh, all right," she said.

"And I want you to swear to me that we will all be safe here with you," Odysseus added. "That you won't use magic against us."

Circe nodded. "I swear." That said, she picked up her wand and a jar of what looked like oil and went out to the sty. Odysseus went with her, and so did I.

Circe dipped the tip of her wand into the oil and began sprinkling it onto the pigs. At once, their snouts shortened, their ears shrank, and their hooves morphed into hands and feet. In no time, they were men again, though they still smelled sort of piggy.

"Thank you for saving us, Odysseus!" they cried.

"We need a bath!" cried one former piggy.

"And not a mud bath, either," said another.

While the ex-pigmen bathed, Odysseus went back to Rylo and the rest of his men to tell them what had happened. I stuck invisibly with him.

"Your fellow crewmen are men again," Odysseus announced. "And Circe has sworn not to use magic against us. Come! Her handmaidens are preparing us a feast."

"Yay!" cried the crewmen.

"Hold it," said Rylo. "I'm not going to any feast at Circe's cottage. Before we know it, we'll all be pigs!"

Odysseus scowled. "I told you we'd be safe," he said. "Do you doubt my words, cousin?"

"You're the one who led us into the cave of the Cyclops," said Rylo. "And look how well *THAT* turned out!"

"Stay here if you like." Odysseus turned and led the rest of his men to the cottage. After a short time, Rylo scurried after them.

I watched the men disappear into the woods. Odysseus had extracted a promise from Circe that she would not turn him or his men into pigs. It seemed as if they'd be safe on her island.

That meant I could go home to my kingdom for a while.

At the time, even I didn't suspect that Circe had other ways to work her magic.

CHAPTER V
GHOST

Ah, it was good to be back home in the Underworld! Good to be doing my kingly duties. And this time I stuck around for such a long stretch that Cerbie finally stopped being spiteful and went back to being the great triple-headed pooch he'd always been.

Each month or so, I'd make a day trip up to earth to see how Odysseus was doing. And every time I checked, I found him and his men living happily on Circe's island. They didn't seem to be in any hurry to get home. I understood. After all they'd been through, why wouldn't they want to hang out for a while in a safe place with great eats?

At the same time, I couldn't help but wish that they'd set sail again. I was ready for Odysseus to make it to back to Ithaca. Once he was home, I could stop worrying about what sort of revenge my bro Po might take on him for blinding Polyphemus. And I could stop worrying about Po turning my kingdom into Water World.

When fall rolled around, Persephone came home. Life in the Underworld was so good that I sort of forgot about checking on Odysseus. In fact, I didn't think about that wily mortal at all.

Then one warm fall evening, Persephone said, "I have a surprise for you, Hades."

"You know I'm not big on surprises, P-phone," I said.

"I've made a picnic supper," Persephone went on. "We're going to eat it beside the Pool of Memory, and I've asked the Furies to join us."

As surprises go, that didn't sound so bad. We headed over to the P of M. Persephone carried a picnic basket, and Cerbie trotted happily at my side. When we reached the spot, I saw that Meg, Tisi, and Alec were already there, sitting under the poplar trees.

The three Furies have been in the universe practically forever, doing odd jobs, most of which involve revenge. They live in their own wing of Villa Pluto, and each night they fly up to earth on their great, black, leathery wings to punish wicked mortals, lashing them with their little whips called scourges. Mortals who aren't nice to their mothers? They get extra lashes.

"Greetings, my avengers!" I said, sitting down next to Tisi on a patch of asphodel while Persephone spread her picnic cloth and began laying out our supper. "What's new with you?"

Tisi smiled, showing her gleaming white fangs. "We just got back from Ithaca," she said.

"Really?" I said. "Did you see Odysseus's wife, Penelope?"

"We didn't," said Meg. She shook her head, riling up the dozens of snakes that she and the other Furies have instead of hair.

"But we saw Telemachus!" said Alec.

"Ah, their son," I said. "I hope he hasn't been mean to his mother."

"Telemachus is a good son," said Tisi.

"But he wants to leave home to search for his father," added Meg.

"And that makes his mother worry!" said Alec.

"Hold it," I said. "How old is Telemachus?"

"He's almost a man now," said Tisi.

"Odysseus has been gone for many years," added Meg.

"Some say Odysseus is dead!" said Alec.

"No, he's alive," I told them. "He and what's left of his crew are chilling with Circe on her island right now, but I'm hoping he'll soon head home."

"Many suitors have come to the palace to woo Penelope," Tisi said.

"Whoever marries her will become king of Ithaca," added Meg.

"The suitors are wicked!" said Alec.

"They loll about Odysseus's palace all day," Tisi put in.

"They eat Odysseus's food and drink his wine," said Meg.

"They are disgusting!" said Alec.

"Let's eat!" called Persephone.

I turned and saw that the goddess of spring had spread out a colorful fall feast on her picnic cloth — roasted purple eggplants and red peppers, pasta salad with yellow tomatoes, and for dessert, blueberry pie.

We all dug in.

* * *

I kept meaning to go see what Odysseus was up to on Circe's island, but days turned into weeks, and weeks turned into months, and somehow I never got around to it.

One afternoon, I was driving my chariot, making the usual rounds of my kingdom. Cerbie was dozing contentedly beside me in the passenger seat. Harley and Davidson were going at a nice slow pace, giving me time to get a good look at everything we passed. I drove around the Underworld traffic circle, and past the Underworld Courthouse. Ghosts stood in an orderly line, waiting to be judged. As I passed Motel Styx, I saw ghosts lined up outside, waiting to check in, but only a few. Nothing that Hypnos and Thanatos couldn't handle. It wasn't a sunny day — it never is in the Underworld — but otherwise things couldn't have been more perfect.

Then suddenly Cerberus's eyes popped open, all six at once. He lifted one head. His second head rose and then the third. He looked around, giving the air a big sniff, sniff, sniff.

"What's up, Cerbie?" I asked.

Cerberus answered with a menacing triple-growl and leaped from my chariot.

"Cerbie! Come back!" I cried.

But the Guard Dog of the Underworld ignored me and raced toward the River Styx.

"Giddy up, steeds!" I called. Harley and Davidson broke into a gallop, and at last we caught up with my dog.

"Cerbie!" I called, but he ran on, so I drove

on after him as he sped along the river bank, all three of his tongues hanging out of his mouths. That dog hadn't gotten this much exercise in centuries!

At last we came to the place where the River Oceanus flows into the River Styx. I slowed my steeds, and now I heard what Cerbie's triple hearing must have picked up earlier — mortal voices.

When mortals die and come down to my kingdom, their ghosts speak in thin, high-pitched tones. But now I heard the deep voices of living, mortal men.

Worse yet, the sounds were coming from the secret back entrance to the Underworld. Persephone, Hermes, and I were the only ones who knew about that secret entrance. How had mortals discovered it?

I rounded a corner and yanked on the reins. "Whoa, steeds!" I cried.

They screeched to a halt, which was a good thing, for right in front of them stood Odysseus and his crew. Cerberus had cornered the whole lot of them and backed them up against a rocky wall.

"Grrr! Grrrrrr! Grrrrrrrrrrrr!" growled Cerbie, baring all three sets of teeth.

"Good doggy, doggy, doggy," Odysseus was saying, trying to calm him. "I have a dog. His name's Argos. I love dogs!"

I shouted, "Cerberus, OFF!"

Cerbie gave me a triple dirty look, but he obeyed.

"You're the best guard dog in the Underworld," I praised him as he slunk off. "Yes, you are, are, are!" The last thing I needed was Cerbie getting all bent out of shape because I'd yelled at him.

I hopped out of my chariot. "Odysseus!" I said. "What in the Underworld are you doing down here?"

At the sight of me, the crewmen cowered against the rock.

"We're all going to die!" shrieked Rylo.

But Odysseus broke into a smile. "Lord Hades!" he cried. "Great to see you."

"How did you get down here?" I asked.

"Circe the sorceress told us the way," said Odysseus.

So much for my secret entrance.

"Circe cast a spell on me," Odysseus went on. "It made me forget all about going home. It made me want to stay with her forever."

So that's why the men stayed so long on that island. I should have guessed that turning men into pigs wasn't Circe's only trick.

"After a year, my men came to me and said they wanted to go home," Odysseus continued. "I went to Circe and asked to be set free. She lifted her spell from me and agreed to let us go, but she warned me of the many perils we will face on our journey home. And she said that before we set sail, we must travel down here to speak with the ghost of the blind prophet, Tiresias of Thebes."

"What for?" I asked.

"Because he can see into the future," Odysseus said. "And only he can tell us what we need to know to reach Ithaca."

I heard the tap of a cane and turned to see the ghost of Tiresias coming toward us.

"You have visitors, Tiresias," I told him.

"Is that you, Lord Hades?" asked the ghost of blind the prophet in his high, ghostly voice. "I've been wanting a word with you. My living quarters down here are not as promised."

I sighed. Ghosts are so ungrateful. Even the ones like Tiresias, who spend their afterlives in beautiful Elysium.

"We'll talk later, Tiresias," I told him. "Right now, you need to advise the mortal, Odysseus."

"Ah, yes!" said the prophet. "I knew this moment would come. Foretold it all." He smiled. "I will speak with you in private, Odysseus," he said, and Odysseus led him away from the others. The crewmen couldn't hear what was said, but with my godly hearing, I took in every word.

"Listen to me, Odysseus," said Tiresias. "Poseidon is boiling mad at you for blinding his son, Polyphemus."

"Duh," said Odysseus.

"He will make your journey home absolutely horrifying!" warned Tiresias.

"He's already done that!" said Odysseus.

"If you and your crew want to get home safely," Tiresias went on, "you must do exactly as I say."

"I'm all ears," said Odysseus.

"Your ship will pass the green-hilled island of Thrinacia," Tiresias said. "This is where the sun god Helios keeps his sacred cattle. Whatever you do, DON'T TOUCH THOSE COWS!"

"Okay," said Odysseus. "Anything else?"

"If you do no harm to Helios's cattle, you and your crew may reach home safely," Tiresias went on. "But remember — don't mess with the cows!"

"We won't," said Odysseus. "Is that it?"

"LEAVE THE COWS ALOOOOOONE!" wailed the ghost.

"All right already!" said Odysseus. "I get it."

Tiresias shook his cane at the mortal hero. "Heed my words, Odysseus!" he cried. "Or all your men shall die horrible deaths!"

"What about . . . me?" said Odysseus.

Tiresias shrugged. "You may survive," he said. "But your homecoming won't be any picnic."

"What does that mean?" cried Odysseus.

"Suitors for your wife's hand have taken over your palace," said Tiresias.

"What?" cried Odysseus. "I'll slay them all!"

"I wouldn't bet on it," said Tiresias. "There are more than a hundred of them and only one of you."

Odysseus's face reddened with anger. "Anything else, prophet?" he growled.

"Yes," said Tiresias. "Even if you do manage to get rid of the suitors, you must still take a long journey by land."

Odysseus groaned loudly.

"You must put an oar over your shoulder and walk from city to city until you meet someone who doesn't know what you're carrying," said Tiresias.

"Everybody knows what an oar is!" said Odysseus.

"Not someone who's never seen the sea," pointed out Tiresias. "When you come to this place, make a sacrifice to Poseidon. Only then will he forgive you."

"This is sooooo complicated," wailed Odysseus.

"Just leave the cows alone," said Tiresias. "That's all I have to say."

The ghost of the old prophet turned and began tapping his way back to Elysium.

I stepped toward Odysseus, half thinking of inviting him to come back to the palace for a cold one. But I wondered — would Po consider that helping? In the end, I said nothing and watched him go back to his men.

"Good luck with the rest of the trip!" I called after him.

Odysseus turned around and gave me a wave.

"Thanks, Hades." He sounded a little down after his chat with Tiresias. "I could really use some good luck."

CHAPTER VI

SEA MONSTERS!

It was spring before I caught up with Odysseus and his crew again. They'd left Circe's island, and I found their ship stalled in the middle of the ocean without so much as a whisper of wind to fill its sails. Once again, the men were rowing.

Po holds a mean grudge, I thought as I landed invisibly on the ship.

Rylo had his head cocked as if listening to something. At last he said, "Does anyone else hear singing?"

"Singing?" cried Odysseus. "It's the Sirens. Stop rowing!"

The crewmen lifted their oars out of the water. The ship bobbed up and down on the waves and I started feeling queasy. I took a few deep breaths. It helped.

Odysseus pulled a parchment-wrapped package out from under his seat. "Circe warned me of this peril," he said, tearing off the wrapping. "She told me all about the Sirens. That's who's singing."

A crewman nodded toward the package. "What's that?" he asked.

"Beeswax," said Odysseus. "Circe gave it to me. You must stuff it in your ears before we get any closer to the Sirens." He began pinching plugs of wax from the block and handing them out to his crew. "Once you've plugged your ears, you must row as fast as you can so we'll pass the Sirens and be out of danger."

"Danger?" said Rylo. "Who are the Sirens?"

"Three goddess sisters who sit on a rocky island and sing," said Odysseus. "Circe says that the Sirens' songs are so beautiful that no sailor who hears their singing can resist diving into the sea and swimming out to their island to be with them."

"What's wrong with that?" cried a crewman.

"Yeah, we could use a little break from this ship," said another.

"Sirens, here we come!" called Rylo.

"Circe also said," Odysseus went on, "that the flowering sea grass surrounding the Sirens' island hides the bones of sailors who swam out and were dashed against the rocky shore."

The men quickly began shoving beeswax into their ears.

"How come you're not plugging your ears, Odysseus?" asked Rylo.

"I want to hear the Sirens' song." Odysseus held out a length of rope. "Quick, cousin! Tie me to the mast. That way I won't be able to dive into the sea when I hear the singing."

How like Odysseus! He wanted to hear the Sirens' song — and he'd come up with a clever way not to pay the price.

Rylo bound him tightly to the mast.

"No matter how I beg, don't untie me," ordered Odysseus.

"I won't," Rylo said, and then he stuffed his own ears with beeswax.

Now the men picked up their oars and rowed as fast as they could to get past the Sirens and their fatal songs.

Being a god, I could easily resist the Sirens' voices. But those three were some fine singers, I had to give them that.

When she was a young goddess, Persephone was good friends with the Sirens, Thea, Pia, and Aggie. At that time, they were three good-looking minor goddesses. Nothing special really, except for their voices.

The first time I met Persephone, she hitched a ride down to the Underworld with me and didn't let her mom, Demeter, know where she was. Demeter freaked out. She went to the Sirens and asked them to look for her daughter. They agreed, and Demeter caused huge bird wings to sprout from their backs so they could fly around the earth, looking for Persephone. Demeter also turned their feet into birdie claws so they could land on tree branches if necessary.

The Sirens flew around the whole earth, searching for Persephone, but they never thought to look for her in the Underworld. At last they returned to Demeter and said they couldn't find her. Demeter was furious. She claimed that they hadn't looked hard enough, that they hadn't flown far enough, and she refused to change the Sirens back into their former minor-goddess selves. Angry, the three spread their mighty wings and flew off to a rocky island. They were powerless to hurt Demeter, so they took out their revenge on men who sailed the sea.

As Odysseus's ship neared their far-away island, I heard the Sirens singing loud and clear:

Odysseus! You are the man!
Swim over to us if you can.
Come closer now, don't make a fuss,
We sing of YOU, Odysseus!
We know you want to hear THAT song.
We'll sing it for you all day long.

"Untie me!" Odysseus bellowed.

"What's that?" yelled the crewman nearest to him.

"CUT ME LOOSE!" Odysseus shouted.

"Whatever you say, captain." The crewman made his way over to him.

"Hurry!" shouted Odysseus. "They're singing a song about ME!"

"What's that?" said the crewman.

"CUT THE ROPES!" shouted Odysseus.

"Ah, the ropes!" the crewman said. "Let me get my knife."

As he searched for his knife, the Sirens sang on:

We know you won the war in Troy,
We know you are the golden boy,
We know Poseidon's mad as heck.
Come on now, O, dive off the deck!

We know the future, yes, we do,
Come closer and you'll know it, too!
We know about Penelope,
We'll tell you all, we guarantee!

We'll tell about Telemachus.
Who knows about your son? Just us!
We know you'd like some news of him —
Come on now, champ, and take that swim!

Odysseus was shouting and pleading for somebody to set him free, but by the time the crewman found his knife, the ship had left the Sirens' rocky island far behind.

"There you go!" said the crewman, cutting the ropes. "Better now?"

Odysseus slid down the mast and sat in a crumpled heap. "I really wanted to hear more of that song about me," he said sadly.

Now that Odysseus was out of danger, I *ZZZZIPPED* over to the Sirens' island and de-helmeted: *FOOP!*

"Good morning, ladies!" I said.

"Hades!" the Sirens cried. They asked me all about Persephone, and I filled them in on our life in the Underworld.

After we'd caught up, Thea said, "Sorry to cut this visit short, but we were just leaving, Lord Hades."

"Oh, going on a trip?" I asked.

"Sort of," Pia said. "An old prophecy has just been fulfilled. It is said that if a mortal man hears our song and lives to tell about it, we Sirens will jump into the sea and disappear."

The Sirens laughed.

"We're going to disappear, all right," said Aggie. "But we're not jumping into the sea. We're flying to Dodona for a couple of centuries, and then on to California."

"California?" I said.

"We know the future," said Thea.

"That's right," said Pia. "We're going to LA, and we're going to become singing sensations!"

"We'll be huge stars!" said Aggie. "No more of these freebie rock concerts."

"But what about . . . I mean, aren't you worried about your wings and . . . everything?" I asked, not wanting to mention the birdie feet. "Do you think the mortals there will accept you?"

"We're talking LA," said Thea.

"You can't be too freaky for LA," added Pia.

"They're gonna love us," said Aggie. She turned to her sisters. "Ready, girls?"

The other two nodded, and as I watched, they spread their wings and took to the air, heading west.

* * *

I helmeted up again — *POOF!* — and *ZIPPED* back to Odysseus's ship. A thick fog had rolled in. Through the mist I saw that the ship was headed for a narrow strip of sea between two huge black rocks. The current in the passage was super swift. Getting that ship through it was going to be like white-water rafting.

"I don't like the looks of this," said a crewman.

The other crewmen nodded and muttered darkly.

"Look! A huge whirlpool!" cried Rylo, pointing toward the sea near the rock to the left. He turned to Odysseus as the ship began to tilt and sway. "Did Circe warn you of *this* peril?"

"She did!" Odysseus shouted over the roar of the rapids. "Beneath that rock lives the sea monster Charybdis. Three times a day she sucks down the sea, creating an enormous whirlpool. And three times a day she vomits the sea up again."

"Woe is us!" cried a crewman.

I feared for Odysseus and his men. Charybdis was one of Po's monstrous daughters. Had Po let her know that Odysseus and his ship were approaching?

"If Charybdis sucks our ship into her whirlpool, none of us will survive!" shouted Odysseus. "We must steer the ship close to the rock on the right side of this narrow passage."

"That's the safe side, right?" yelled a crewman.

"Absolutely!" called Odysseus. "Remember, men, row close to the right side!"

I was starting to drosis. If the crewmen steered the ship to the right side of the channel, they'd meet another horrible sea monster — Scylla, a six-headed, man-eating dragon who dwelt in a cave on the opposite side of the narrow passage from Charybdis.

I turned and saw Odysseus putting on his armor. He thrust his sword into his belt. Clearly Circe had warned him about the peril of Scylla. And now he was armored up, ready to do battle with the six-headed monster!

Rylo frowned. "If it's so safe, why are you putting on armor, Odysseus?" he asked.

"Just in case," said Odysseus. He grabbed a spear.

Suddenly Rylo screamed, "What's THAT?"

THAT was Scylla. She'd poked her six heads out of her cave. Spying the ship, she extended her six long, snake-like necks until her six hideous heads hovered over the ship. Scylla lowered her heads. She opened her six large mouths, each one filled with rows and rows of jagged dragon teeth.

Odysseus hurled his spear at the dragon! He slashed at her necks with his sword! But nothing stopped her. Six dragon heads darted down and snatched up six unlucky crewmen.

I closed my godly eyes.

"ROW!" Odysseus shouted to his crew. "ROW!" He didn't want that dragon coming back for seconds.

Those men rowed faster than any mortals had ever rowed before or since, and in no time, they were back out on the open sea.

"Oh, horror!" cried Rylo. "Did Circe not warn you of *THAT* peril?"

Odysseus shrugged. "She must've forgotten."

How easily a lie rolled off Odysseus's tongue! Rylo and the other men could tell he was lying, too. But no one blamed him. If he'd told them the truth as they'd entered the narrow passage — that six of them must die in Scylla's jaws in order to save the rest of the crew — how could he have asked his men to row on? He'd made the right call.

"The wind is picking up," Odysseus said, changing the subject. "Hoist the sails, men. Onward to Ithaca!"

Chapter VII
SACRED COWS

Unseen, I stayed with Odysseus and his surviving crewmen as they sailed under a steady breeze for many days with no land in sight. After a while, I got my sea legs and stopped feeling sick. And then came a windless day. The men picked up their oars and began to row. Just as I was thinking that I might want to *ZIP* off for a while, Rylo shouted, "Land ahoy!"

"Hurray!" the crewmen cheered. They rowed faster.

As the ship neared a hilly green island,

sounds of cattle mooing filled the air. I could tell from the *uh-oh* expression on Odysseus's face that he was thinking about Tiresias's warning.

"So!" Odysseus said as the men rowed toward the island. "This must be Thrinacia. We can't stop here."

"What? Why not?" cried the crew.

"Trust me on this," said Odysseus.

"But if we drop anchor at this island, we can feast on the cattle," said Rylo.

"No. We can't," said Odysseus. "Anyway, we don't need cattle. We still have plenty of the food that Circe gave us."

"But it's all that salad-y stuff," said a crewman.

"And fruit and grains and nuts," complained another.

"We need meat!" cried a third.

"Meat! Meat! Meat!" the men chanted.

"Quiet!" shouted Odysseus. "I'm the captain, and I say we row on to another island."

"But there's no other island in sight!" said Rylo.

"I'm not rowing any more," growled a crewman.

"Me neither! Me neither!" cried the others.

Poor Odysseus! He had a mutiny on his hands. "Have it your way," Odysseus said at last. "We'll land on Thrinacia. But you must swear to eat only Circe's food and leave those cows alone."

"Yeah, yeah, we swear," called the men, and in under an hour, they were making camp on the beach in Thrinacia.

That night, after dining on green salads topped with figs and herbed goat cheese, the men rolled up in their blankets on the beach, muttering that dinner hadn't filled them up.

I checked the sky and saw that clouds were blowing in, covering the moon and stars. Lightning flashed in the distance. Thunder rumbled. Zeus was bringing in a storm.

I looked at the sleeping sailors. They'd been through many a storm. They could handle another. They'd sworn to Odysseus to leave Helios's cattle alone. Everything seemed to be all right, and so I *ZZZZIPPED* off, leaving the slumbering crew in the gentle rain that had started to fall.

* * *

By the time I got back to Villa Pluto, I was beat. I'd never worn my Helmet of Darkness for such a long stretch in my whole immortal life as I had these past few years, chasing Odysseus around the globe. Being invisible for days on end took a toll.

When I walked into our living quarters, Persephone called, "Is that you, Hades?"

"Who else?" I called back, and she hurried into the den.

"Welcome home!" she said, hugging me. "You look a little tired."

"I am," I said, flopping down onto my La-Z-god. I levered it into the foot-up position. "Keeping tabs on Odysseus is not so easy." I managed a smile. "How are you doing, P-phone?"

"I'm great," she said. "But I'm a little worried about Cerberus."

"What's wrong with him?" I cried, jumping out of my La-Z-god. "Does he need to see the Underworld vet?"

"No, he just mopes around when you're away," Persephone said. "He's lonely, Hades."

I searched the palace for that dog, and finally I found him under Hypnos's bed. I lured him into the den with a bunch of Luv-a-Liver Treats, sat down on the floor beside him, and gave him a major belly rub.

"I'm here, Cerbie," I said. "From now on it's you and me, pooch."

But the minute I ran out of treats, that dog slunk off to who knows where, and I didn't see him for the rest of the day.

The whole next week he refused to ride shotgun with me when I drove to meet Charon's water taxi. He wasn't by my side on the banks of the River Styx when I greeted each new batch of ghosts, either.

Cerbie was mad at me — again.

Happy as I was to be home, a lingering worry about Odysseus and his crew nagged at me. They'd been through bad times before, but my scalp had started prickling, and I couldn't shake the feeling that something worse was about to happen to them.

In the evenings, to distract myself, I tuned into wrestling on TV. But not even my favorite wrestler, Eagle-Eye Cyclops, could take my mind off Odysseus. I kept switching to the Weather Channel. Not that I believed half the stuff that Weather Seer predicted. Still, I couldn't help but notice that for weeks on end he kept saying that a huge storm was holding steady over the island of Thrinacia.

The last thing I wanted to do was put on my Helmet of Darkness again, but I couldn't rest until I'd checked on Odysseus. So once more I left my dog howling behind me and drove up to earth. I clamped on my Helmet — *POOF!* — and *ZIPPED* straight to Thrinacia.

For a change, the Weather Seer had it right. A terrible storm was churning up enormous waves all around the island. The huge breakers made it impossible for Odysseus and his crew to sail away.

I made my invisible way to Odysseus's waterlogged campsite. In spite of the pouring rain, a crewman had managed to start a sputtering fire.

Rylo trudged into camp. He was thin as a rail. "This is all I caught today," he said, holding up a scrawny bird. He turned to Odysseus, who sat hunkered down by the fire. "We can't live like this much longer," he said. "We must kill a cow!"

"No," Odysseus said firmly. "The storm will pass, and we will be on our way."

I'd sworn not to help Odysseus. But I couldn't stand by while he and his crew slowly starved to death.

ZZZZZZZZZZZZZZZZIP!

I landed on Mount Olympus, ripped off my Helmet — *FOOP!* — and hurried to the Great Hall to have a talk with Zeus.

I found him sitting on his throne while a grooming nymph painted his toenails.

"Hello, Zeus," I said.

Zeus frowned up at me. "Hades!" he growled. "What do you want?"

"What's with the giant storm you've got going over Thrinacia?" I asked him.

Zeus grinned. "The years haven't slowed me down one bit, have they, Hades?" he said. "That was my biggest storm ever!"

"Was?" I said. "You mean it's over?"

"For now." Zeus waggled his hairy toes at me. "You like this color? Midnight blue."

"Very nice," I said. "Did Po talk you into sending that storm?"

"Nobody talks me into anything!" boomed Zeus. "I'm King of the gods! I do whatever I want! Besides," he added, "Po's gone off to Ethiopia, where he's being wined and dined by his worshippers. He's been there for ages, having the time of his life." He frowned. "Don't smudge the polish!" he barked at the grooming nymph, who was trying to position his left foot under a dryer.

"Odysseus is sorry about blinding Po's son," I said. "He feels bad, and —"

"Mind your own beeswax, Hades!" Zeus cut me off. He raised his right foot onto the stool, and the nymph began painting tiny lightning bolts on top of the blue polish.

Just then, someone shouted, "Zeus! Zeus!"

"How am I supposed to get my toes done with all the racket around here?" grumbled Zeus.

Helios, the Titan sun god, raced into the Great Hall, his purple robe billowing out behind him. His golden crown shone as brightly as the sun. "Odysseus and his men have slain my cattle!" he cried.

My godly heart sank. The worst had happened.

"My lovely cowwwwwws!" Helios howled. "My bovine beauties! Gone!"

"They're just cows, Helios," said Zeus.

"J-j-just cows?" sputtered Helios. "Hear me, Zeus! Every morning before dawn, I ride my sun chariot into the dark heavens. All day, I work and toil to pull the sun across the sky. I keep an iron grip on the reins of my steeds. I can never let up! It's a grueling job. No lunch break for the sun god. No coffee break. No chatting by the water cooler. I don't get home until way after sunset, but when I do, I like to walk among my cattle in the moonlight and hear their gentle mooing. Mooooo! Moooooo! Mooooo!"

Helios threw back his head and mooed his heart out. While he did, Zeus spread his toes and admired his pedi, but I listened politely to the mooing. I knew better than to make the sun god angry. That deity can send a spark anywhere in the universe and start a blazing fire. He's a dangerous enemy. And Odysseus was about to find out just how dangerous he was.

At last Helios stopped mooing and went on with his tale. "I finally get back to my island and what do I find? Six of my cows, butchered!" He wiped a tear from his sunburned cheek. "I'm a vegetarian," he added. "I hate the thought of eating meat. And I come home to find a bunch of lowly mortals grilling steaks and burgers made from my cows!" His eyes flashed wildly. "Those mortals must pay for their crimes! Or never again will I pull the sun across the sky. I shall drive my flaming chariot down to the Underworld and stay there for eternity!"

"Hold it, Helios!" I said quickly. "Sunshine belongs to the mortals on earth, not to the shades below."

"I want revenge!" shrieked Helios.

"And you shall have it!" cried Zeus. He turned to his grooming nymph. "Are my left toes dry?"

The nymph nodded, and Zeus leaped to his feet, shouting, "Somebody bring my Bucket o' Bolts, on the double!"

Another nymph hurried into the room carrying the enormous bucket. She put it down in front of Zeus. He grabbed the bucket and strode to the open side of the Great Hall where we gods look down upon the earth. Helios and I were right behind him.

Looking through a break in the clouds, I saw a tiny ship bobbing on the ocean. Odysseus and his crew must have set sail as soon as the storm around Thrinacia ended, hoping to escape Helios's wrath.

Zeus snatched up a bolt, drew back his

massive arm — and I'm not talking muscle here — and threw. The thunderbolt fluttered down, down, down without picking up much speed. But sadly Zeus's aim was true. The white-hot bolt made a direct hit on Odysseus's ship.

CRRRRRACK!

The ship split in two and burst into flames.

Zeus tossed more bolts at the burning ship just for fun. The skies roared with thunder.

As I watched, the ship splintered into pieces. Some parts of it were carried off by waves. Others sank. Poor Odysseus! He'd tried his best to keep his men from eating Helios's cattle, but he couldn't do it. Now he'd lost his ship . . . and his life.

See you in the Underworld, Odysseus, I thought.

"Thanks, Zeus," said Helios. "That was vengeance with a capital V." He turned and stomped out of the Great Hall.

"Zeus," I said, "I thought you admired Odysseus."

"I do!" he said. "Er . . . did. He was my kind of mortal! Always ready with a trick or a scam.

Never a big stickler for the truth. But what could I do, Hades? I can't have the sun god going on strike." He looked down at his feet and smiled. "Even my toes say thunder god. Grooming nymph!" he shouted, walking back toward his throne. "Let's finish the T-bolts!"

I took a last look down to where the ship had been. What was that tiny speck bobbing among the waves?

I leaned forward and squinted. It was a head! Could it belong to Odysseus?

I didn't want to give Zeus a clue what I'd seen, or he'd hurl more bolts.

"See you, Zeus," I said with a wave.

"Not if I see you first, Hades!" shouted Zeus.

I heard him laughing and snorting over his stupid joke as I put on my Helmet — *POOF!* — and chanted the *ZIP!* code for Thrinacia.

* * *

I circled Thrinacia in Hover Mode, treading air the way we gods can do, as I searched the sea below. Hovering can be tricky, especially if it's windy out, but I managed to say aloft until I caught sight of the shipwreck survivor. I saw that he'd salvaged some rope and was lashing a piece of the ship's mast to what was left of the keel.

I smiled. Had to be Odysseus.

I'd sworn on the River Styx not to help that mortal, but as I watched him making his raft, I wondered, what had I been so worried about? Odysseus was doing just fine on his own.

Then, quite suddenly, the West Wind died down and the South Wind picked up. It began blowing Odysseus back the way he'd come. Back toward Scylla and Charybdis!

Odysseus realized what was happening and started paddling like mad with the only oars he had — his hands. This time, he kept to the side of the narrow passage closest to Charybdis. When the monster began to swallow the sea, Odysseus paddled near the shore. Just as the swirling waters were about to pull him down, he heaved himself up and grabbed onto a tree branch sticking out from a craggy rock. A second later, his raft was sucked down in Charybdis's sickening swirl.

The poor mortal clutched that tree branch as if his life depended on it, which, of course, it did. Hours went by. But Odysseus clung on like a monkey, waiting for Charybdis to cough up his raft again. How his arms must have ached! His hands must have been scraped raw! But he held on and on.

At last Charybdis threw up the sea again, and with it, the raft. Odysseus released his grip on the branch. He splashed into the churning water, swam to his raft, and rolled on. I watched as he started paddling with his hands again, making very little progress on the vast and choppy sea.

Chapter VIII
CALYPSO

For nine days and nights, every time I checked on Odysseus, I found him paddling or drifting on that raft. He hardly slept. All he'd had to eat were a few fish he'd managed to catch with his hands. I could see the poor guy's ribs!

Odysseus was barely alive when, on the tenth day, the ocean spat him out onto the shore of yet another island. I descended onto the island and looked down at the poor mortal as he lay on the beach, unconscious. He was bruised and battered. His clothing was little more than rags, hardly covering him. I could see the long white boar scar on his thigh.

I hung invisibly around waiting to see if Odysseus would be rescued. Before long, a goddess with a golden glow stepped out of the woods and I recognized Calypso. She was a Titan's daughter, a minor goddess, but a very powerful one. Except for her servants, she lived alone in a cave on Ogygia Island.

Calypso's golden braids shone in the sunlight as she walked down the beach with her serving maids. When she came to the place where Odysseus lay sleeping on the sand, she stopped, and said to her attendants, "A stranger has washed up onto our shore. Carry him to my cave. We shall show him hospitality, as decreed by Zeus."

All my godly instincts told me that Odysseus's life was no longer in danger, but I'd been wrong before. And Calypso had a reputation for casting dangerous spells.

I needed more information before I left Odysseus entirely in her care, which is why I decided to pay a visit to some ladies who could tell me what I needed to know.

ZZZZZZZZZZZZZIP!

I touched down on a hillside high above Sparta. Close to the spot where I'd landed sat three white-robed sisters, chatting in an open-air shelter.

"Greetings, Hades!" one of the sisters called before I'd even taken off my Helmet.

FOOP!

"Greetings, Fates!" I said. "Good to see you."

"We know this isn't a social call," said fair-haired Clotho. As always, she had her little spinning wheel on her lap and was spinning out the threads of mortal fates.

"That's right," said the raven-haired Lachesis as she measured the threads her sister wove. "We know why you've come."

"To find out about Odysseus!" squealed their redheaded sister, Atropos. "And whether he's ready for a — snip!" She held up the shiny silver scissors that she used to cut the threads of life when a mortal's time on earth was up.

"I knew you'd know, my Fates," I said. Even for a major god like me, talking to these three was a mind-bending experience. They knew every move I was going to make, every word I was about to say. "Tell me, fair sisters," I went on, "is Odysseus safe on Calypso's island?"

"Oh, yes," said Clotho, spinning as she spoke. "Calypso, of the lovely braids, can be a dangerous enemy, but she'll be crazy about Odysseus."

"She'll want that mortal to stay with her forever," added Lachesis, measuring the threads. "She's even going to offer to make him immortal."

"No snip," put in Atropos. "Ever!" As she said it, she cut some other poor mortal's thread. *Snip!*

"And what will Odysseus say?" I asked.

"He'll say no," said Clotho. "He'll tell her that he wishes to return home to Ithaca. But even so, Calypso will see to it that he stays with her for seven years."

"Seven years!" I exclaimed. "That's a big chunk of a mortal life."

"True," said Lachesis. "And every day for seven years, Odysseus will sit high on a cliff, looking out to sea, thinking of Penelope and Telemachus."

Odysseus was full of tricks, but I liked hearing that when push came to shove, he was loyal to his wife and son.

"He will search the sea for a passing ship on which he might catch a ride home," said Atropos.

"So in a way, Odysseus will be Calypso's prisoner," I said.

"That's right," said Lachesis, measuring away.

"It's a very nice prison, though," added Clotho. "Lots of grapevines growing all around and crystal clear springs for swimming."

"Do you want to know about Telemachus?" asked Lachesis.

"His mother wishes he would act less like a boy and more like a man," said Atropos.

"Telemachus has sailed off to look for his father," said Clotho, untangling some of the threads she'd spun.

"We can tell you about Penelope, too," said Lachesis.

"Has Penelope taken another husband?" I asked.

"No!" shouted all the Fates.

"But she has many suitors," said Clotho.

"One hundred and eight!" said Atropos. "But who's counting?" She laughed.

"And will Odysseus ever come home to Penelope?" I asked.

"Enough with the questions, Hades!" cried Lachesis. "We've told you too much already."

"No, wait!" I cried. "I have something else to ask you. Something important!"

"We know," said Atropos.

"It's about Cerberus," said Lachesis.

"You want to know why he's so mad when you go away and leave him," said Clotho.

"Exactly, my Fates," I said.

"Think about it, Hades!" said Atropos.

"You'll figure it out," said Lachesis.

"Nice talking to you!" said Clotho, still spinning.

I could see they'd told me all they were going to tell.

"Thanks for everything, my Fates," I said, trying to sound gracious.

"Tell Persephone hello from us!" said Atropos.

"And tell the Furies to stop by one of these nights," added Lachesis. "We haven't seen our cousins for millennia."

"I'll give them your message," I said.

"We know you will, Hades!" called Clotho. "We know it!"

POOF!

ZZZZZZZZZZZZZZZZIP!

* * *

We immortals don't pay much attention to the passing of time. What's time to us? Nothing! When I learned that Odysseus would spend seven years on Ogygia Island, I stopped worrying about our hero. It was his fate to spend that time with Calypso, and there was nothing I could do about it. And as the days and weeks and months went by, I was busy down in my kingdom, and I stopped thinking about Odysseus.

And then one day a new batch of ghosts arrived in my kingdom, fresh from some earthly battlefield.

That made me think back to the days when my kingdom was teeming with ghosts from the Trojan War, and that made me think of the war's greatest hero, Odysseus.

I began to wonder how he was doing up there on Ogygia Island, and I decided to drive up to earth and *ZZZZZIP!* on over to see for myself.

I touched down on the beach where I'd left Odysseus years before, and started invisibly up the wooded path that led to Calypso's cave. I caught a glimpse of someone ahead of me on the path. Someone wearing winged sandals.

"Hermes?" I called, de-helmeting. *FOOP!*

He turned around. "Hades!" he exclaimed.

"Taking a day off from your bus route?" I asked.

"I had to, Hades," said Hermes, and we began walking up the path together. "Athena's been complaining to Zeus about Calypso keeping Odysseus prisoner for so long."

"Athena?" I said. "Why does she care?"

"You know, Athena's the goddess of wisdom and Odysseus is plenty smart, so he's a big favorite of hers," said Hermes. "Plus, every day, Odysseus calls out to her and begs her to help him get home to Ithaca. And there's nothing Athena loves more than a begging mortal."

"Too true," I agreed.

"Though with a beautiful minor goddess to keep him company," Hermes added, "and all of her serving maids — who are great cooks, by the way — things could be a lot worse for Odysseus."

"And they have been," I said. "He lost all twelve of his ships and all of his men."

Hermes nodded. "That mortal has really suffered," he said. "That's why Athena wants to help him out. She's finally convinced Zeus to command Calypso to let Odysseus go. I'm here to tell her."

"Whoa," I said. "I'm glad I don't have to deliver *that* message."

"Tell me about it." Hermes rolled his eyes. "Calypso's going to have a cow." He turned to me. "Hades, it was you who called and told me to go help Odysseus when Circe was about to turn him into a pig, wasn't it?"

"What are you talking about?" I muttered. "Look, here we are at Calypso's cave," I added quickly. "Good luck delivering your message."

I put my Helmet back on — *POOF!* — and sat invisibly beside the mouth of the cave, listening to Hermes tell Calypso that it was time for her to let Odysseus go home.

"You must be joking, Hermes!" cried Calypso. "I found Odysseus lying half dead on my beach. I fed him. I nursed him back to health. I've even offered to make him an immortal."

"Word has it that he's turned you down," said Hermes.

"He's thinking about it," said Calypso.

"Which is weird," said Hermes.

"Totally," said Calypso. "What mortal doesn't want to live forever?"

Hermes shrugged. "Anyway, Calypso,

Odysseus has been with you for seven years," he went on. "Now Zeus commands you to let him go so he can live out the years he has left at home."

Calypso sighed loudly. "Hermes," she said, "nobody wears winged sandals anymore. They are so last century."

"Do as Zeus commands, Calypso," Hermes said, and then I heard his little wings beating as he made his getaway.

I hung invisibly around until Calypso came out of her cave. She headed for a nearby hill and started climbing. I climbed right behind her.

At the top of the hill, there was Odysseus, sitting on a rock and looking out to sea just as Lachesis had predicted.

"Odysseus," said Calypso, putting a hand on his shoulder, "it's time for you to go home."

Odysseus turned toward her. "No kidding?"

"No kidding," said Calypso. "I shall give you tools to build yourself a ship, and I shall fill it with good food and good wine," she added. "I shall weave you a sail, and when you are ready to leave, I shall send winds to fill it."

"Yahoooo!" shouted Odysseus, leaping to his feet. He ran down the hill, whooping and cheering, leaving poor, sad Calypso to follow slowly behind.

I stayed around for a while after that and saw that Calypso did as she had promised. She gave Odysseus carpenters' tools, and he cut down trees and began building his ship.

In addition to hammers, nails, and saws, Calypso must have given Odysseus some magical help, too, because it took him only four days to build the ship.

It didn't take Calypso long to weave Odysseus a fine sail, either. Then, as promised, she filled the hulls of his ship with wine and food. Finally, she gave him a gold-trimmed tunic and cloak and a pair of gold-trimmed sandals to wear on his voyage to Ithaca.

"Whoa, this stuff's heavy," said Odysseus, taking the clothes. "Thanks, Calypso. I'll make a big splash arriving home in this getup."

Odysseus put on his new gold-trimmed clothes and sandals. Then he shoved off in his ship and hoisted his sail. Calypso stood on the beach, waving, with tears streaming down her cheeks.

"Goodbye, Odysseus!" she called. "Farewell!"

Odysseus's sail caught the wind that Calypso sent, and his ship began to speed over the waves, heading east toward Ithaca. He never even looked back.

Once he was on his way, I ducked back down to the Underworld and stayed for a couple of weeks.

The next time I checked on that mortal, he'd made amazing progress.

I landed invisibly on Odysseus's ship as dawn was creeping into the sky. In the light of the new day, Odysseus spotted a hilly island in the distance. He checked his course.

"That's gotta be Ithaca," he murmured to himself. "Awright! I'm almost home!"

CHAPTER IX
ANGRY SEA GOD

With Calypso's steady wind blowing, I didn't feel one bit seasick as Odysseus steered his ship straight for his own beloved island. That mortal had been in Troy for ten years. And it had taken him almost that long to get this close to his home. No way was I going anywhere until he stepped onto dry land in Ithaca.

As we approached the hilly island, I heard a shrill shrieking sound. I turned to see what it was, and I couldn't believe my godly eyes. It was Po! His mutant seahorses were bouncing his sea chariot over the waves at a tremendous speed. Any minute, he'd catch up with Odysseus's ship!

ZZZZZZZZZZZIP!

I landed in the speeding sea chariot with a whiplash-inducing jolt.

FOOP!

"Po, it's been a while!" I shouted over the screeching seahorses. "How was Ethiopia?"

"Don't try to distract me, Hades!" Po shouted back. "I know you've been helping Odysseus. I'm here to deal with him once and for all." He shot me a dirty look. "And when I'm done with him, it's your turn! Your kingdom is gonna be Floodsville!"

"Bro, I haven't helped Odysseus!" I yelled as dark clouds began to gather overhead. "I've kept track of him, yes. But I haven't helped him. No way. I swore to you I wouldn't, and I've kept my word."

Maybe in a court of law he could get me on technicalities, but I spoke the truth.

"Mold, Hades!" Po shouted. "Black mold seeping out from under your throne. Brown mold creeping over that recliner you lounge around in watching those wrestling matches. Persephone is going to pack her bags and move back up to earth for good!"

The winds picked up. They howled and swirled every which way, rocking the sea chariot like a bucking bronco. My stomach lurched.

"Enough vengeance, Po!" I shouted. I was going to be sick. I kept talking, hoping the feeling would pass. "Odysseus has been at sea for years, trying to get home. He's lost all his ships, all his men. He's got nothing!"

"And now?" cried Po. "He's about to become fish food!"

The winds raged with hurricane force. Through the spray, I saw Odysseus's ship tilt crazily to the side. A huge wave crashed onto the sail, pulling the ship down. The mast cracked as it hit the water, and Odysseus was blown overboard.

"That's the end of him, Hades!" Po shouted. "Good riddance!" He pulled on his reins, turning his team away from the shipwreck, and sped off.

I jammed on my Helmet — *POOF!* — and went into Hover Mode. Was my bro right? After all Odysseus had been through, was he going to end up on the bottom of the ocean just off the coast of Ithaca?

Po's storm wasn't letting up. I searched the sea for Odysseus, but he was nowhere to be found. All the heavy, gold-trimmed clothing that Calypso had given him must have sunk him fast.

I sighed. Penelope would never know how close her husband had been to coming home. Telemachus would search forever and never find his father. Neither of them would ever see Odysseus again. I'd see him, of course, but only as a shade in the Underworld.

Suddenly, a head popped up among the waves.

Odysseus! I should never have given up on him! He spat out a mouthful of seawater and grabbed onto some wreckage from his ship.

But the storm winds were still whirling. How long could he last? If ever a mortal needed help, Odysseus needed it now.

I'd promised not to help him, but I'd never sworn not to call for help.

"INO!" I shouted into the winds. "A SAILOR IS DROWNING!"

Ino had once been a mortal woman. She and her husband had offended Hera, and in a fit of temper, Hera caused the husband to go mad. In his crazed state, the poor man tried to kill his wife. To escape him, Ino leaped into the sea. Some sea goddesses took pity on her, saved her from drowning, and changed her into one of them. Now her mission was to help sailors in distress.

"INO!" I called again. But the only answer I heard was the howling winds. Now the clouds opened and rain poured down in buckets.

"INO!" I called a third time, and almost before her name faded from the air, I caught sight of her head bobbing up between two huge waves. Her long blond hair floated around her face as her sky-blue eyes searched the sea.

I had on my Helmet. Ino couldn't see me. But as I'd hoped, she caught sight of Odysseus hanging desperately onto a piece of wood. She swam toward him.

"Shed those heavy clothes, sailor!" she called. "Put this on!" She tossed him her scarf. It looked like an ordinary scarf made of sea grass, but in fact it was a magical life preserver.

Odysseus caught the scarf.

"When you are safely on shore, look toward the land and throw the scarf back into the surf," said Ino. "It will find me." Then she disappeared beneath the waves.

Hanging onto timbers from his ship, Odysseus struggled out of his weighty golden clothes. He knotted Ino's scarf around his waist and started swimming. He couldn't have known where he was headed, yet on he swam. Every now and then, he'd float on his back to catch his breath. And then the poor mortal flipped back over and started swimming again. And all I could do was hover over him, watching.

At last, an island came into view. Seeing land, Odysseus began swimming faster.

Go Odysseus! I silently cheered.

As he neared the island, he saw that the rocky shore was pounded by a strong surf. If he tried to swim to land, the waves would toss him onto the rocks over and over again.

But Odysseus wasn't going to let that stop him. When he saw the danger ahead, he turned and swam parallel to the land. At last he came to the mouth of a river flowing into the sea. With what little strength he had left, he swam for the river. When he reached it, he pulled himself up to stand in the shallow water.

"Thank you, sea goddess," he managed as he untied Ino's scarf from his waist. Then he looked toward the land and tossed the scarf back into the waves.

Exhausted and shivering, the poor naked mortal staggered onto the shore. How I wished I could give him the extra robe I always carry in my wallet! But I could only watch helplessly as Odysseus trudged on beside the river. When he reached a pair of low-growing olive trees, he crawled between them, covered himself with their leafy boughs, and fell into a deep sleep.

Chapter X
WILD MAN

While Odysseus slept, I walked invisibly beside the river, hoping to figure out what island he'd landed on this time, and whether he'd be safe here.

The river led to a city. Fine houses with flower gardens, fig trees, and grapevines lined the streets. Clearly my Persephone had been here!

I walked until I came to a white stone palace. Its gates stood wide open with no guards in sight. A sign over the gates read: WELCOME TO THE ROYAL PALACE OF PHAEACIA.

Ah, Phaeacia! So that's where Odysseus had washed up.

The Phaeacian people had once lived on an island near Po's one-eyed sons. As you can imagine, those cannibal Cyclopes weren't the greatest neighbors, so one day the Phaeacians gathered up all that they owned and sailed off to find the most remote island in the world to make a new home for themselves. And this island was the spot they'd found.

I walked back the way I'd come beside the river, thinking.

The good news was that Odysseus had landed on an island inhabited by noble people known for throwing great parties and cooking up amazing feasts.

The bad news was that the Phaeacians disliked strangers. Oh, they were friendly and trusting among themselves, but few ships ever reached their faraway island, and they weren't used to seeing strange faces. Would they welcome Odysseus? I wasn't so sure.

I'd nearly reached the olive trees where our

hero lay sleeping when a series of shrieks filled the air, and I saw three serving maids running toward a young noblewoman. They were screaming their heads off.

And then I spotted Odysseus. He'd stuck his head out from between the olive branches and was trying to keep the rest of himself hidden by the leaves. His thin face was burned red from the sun. Bright white sea salt was caked on his hair and beard. No wonder those serving maids were screaming!

"We were looking for your ball, princess!" cried one of the maids, gasping for breath. "And we came upon a wild man hiding in the olive trees!"

"Take me to him," the young woman said, showing no fear. "We must offer him hospitality."

This was a good sign! Maybe the Phaeacians would welcome Odysseus after all.

The serving maids shook their heads. They were too frightened to go near the wild man again, but they pointed to where he was hiding.

As the young noblewoman approached him,

Odysseus called, "Hello there! Are you a goddess or a mortal?"

I tried not to laugh. After all these years at war and at sea, he still had the old Odysseus charm.

"I'm guessing you're a goddess," Odysseus went on. "You're strong, yet graceful. Let me think . . . Artemis, goddess of the hunt. Am I right?"

The young woman smiled and shook her head. "I'm no goddess," she said.

"Well, if you're a mortal," Odysseus said, "surely you're a princess. "

"True," the young woman said. "I am Princess Nausicaa, daughter of King Alcinous and Queen Arete of Phaeacia."

Odysseus bowed, but he didn't give his name. Even as he was being welcomed by a princess, he was cautious not to reveal too much.

Princess Nausicaa clapped for her serving maids. "Bring water for the stranger," she said. "And those little cakes we brought for our snack."

Odysseus gulped down the water. He ate all

the cakes, too, but of course they weren't nearly enough to fill him up.

"Thank you, princess," he said. "I have been tossed onto your shores, having suffered mightily on my travels, and you have shown me great kindness."

"That is my duty," the princess said. "You can bathe in the river, stranger," she added, blushing a little. "I will have my handmaids bring a robe and more food and water and leave them on the riverbank for you."

"Thank you, princess," said Odysseus.

"When you have washed and dressed," the princess went on, "walk beside the river until you come to our city. Walk quickly and speak to no one. My family obeys Zeus's decree to show hospitality to strangers, but most Phaeacians are suspicious and will not treat you kindly."

Odysseus nodded. "Good to know."

"When you reach the palace, go inside," the princess said. "In the great hall, look for a noblewoman spinning purple yarn. That will be my mother, Queen Arete. Throw yourself down at her feet and say you are a stranger. Ask her for whatever you wish and she will give it to you."

Odysseus smiled. "I have washed up on a fortunate shore indeed, princess," he said. "I shall do as you say."

The princess and her maids turned and walked away.

When he was alone, Odysseus waded into the river and washed the sea salt from his hair and beard. He dried himself in the sun and put on the robe that the maids had left him.

As he began to eat the bread, cheese, and olives that the maids had brought, it occurred to me that I hadn't spoken to Odysseus since he'd come down to my kingdom to talk to Tiresias. I couldn't see any harm in appearing to him now. Besides, I was dying to take off my Helmet.

FOOP!

Odysseus looked up. "Hades!" he cried. "What a surprise!" Then his face fell. "I'm not going to die now, am I? After surviving monsters and shipwrecks, I'd really hate to end it all choking on an olive pit."

"I'm the ruler of the Underworld, Odysseus, not the god of death." I said. Why could mortals never get that straight? I sat down beside him on the riverbank.

"I've been through it, Hades," Odysseus said. He told me about his narrow escapes, and about his men slaying Helios's cattle. "All I want to do is go home," he added with a sigh.

"Maybe the queen will give you a ship and you can sail home," I told him.

Odysseus frowned. "How do you know about the queen, Hades?" he asked. "Are you pals with her?"

"Oh, you know how queens are," I said quickly, hoping that the wily mortal wouldn't figure out that I'd been listening in. "They love to grant wishes."

"I am going to ask the queen for a ship," Odysseus said, flashing a grin. "And I bet she'll give me one, too."

For someone who only hours before had crawled out of the ocean like a dying sea slug, Odysseus was full of his old confidence. And I have to say, considering all the ordeals he'd been though, he cleaned up very well.

Odysseus rose to his feet. "See you around, Hades," he said, and he began walking toward the city.

"Good luck to you, Odysseus!" I called after him.

I watched until he disappeared around a bend. He seemed carefree, but I was worried about him. The princess had warned him that some Phaeacians would not treat him kindly. What they'd do if they saw him walking beside the river was anybody's guess.

Remembering what Hermes had told me about Athena being fond of Odysseus, I got out my phone and punched in her number.

"This is Athena, goddess of wisdom, war, and weaving," she said.

"Hi, Athena. It's me, Hades."

"Oh, Hades, I'm relieved it's you and not those crackpot Centaurs who've been prank calling me," she said. "I don't think it's one bit funny."

Having a sense of humor was not Athena's strong point.

"You were a big fan of Odysseus's during the Trojan War, right?" I asked.

"I was," said Athena. "Still am. So?"

"So Po is making his trip home from the war really horrendous," I said.

"Poseidon is such a nincompoop!" Athena shouted into the phone. "The way he tried to take Athens, my namesake city, for himself. Ohhhhhhh, it still makes my ichor boil."

"I hear you," I told her. "So, Athena, Odysseus could use some help. I can't help him myself. Long story, but in a nutshell, I had to swear to Po that I wouldn't."

"What?" cried Athena. "That god of the seas is totally out of control."

"Don't I know it," I said. "Anyway, if you'd give Odysseus a little assist, that would be super. He's just washed up onto the shores of Phaeacia, and you know how suspicious of strangers some Phaeacians can be."

"I know! I know! I wasn't born yesterday,

Hades," said Athena. "Well, I wasn't born at all, really. I emerged from Zeus's head fully grown and wearing my suit of armor and my helmet." She paused. "Uh, what were we talking about?"

"You're going to help Odysseus," I told her. "You're going to get him safely to the palace to see Queen Arete."

We exchanged a few more barbs about Po and hung up. I smiled. Athena was on the case!

I helmeted up — *POOF!* — and caught up with Odysseus. As he neared the city, a maiden carrying a water jug approached him. I knew right away who she was. Athena didn't have the greatest sense of humor, as I've said, but like Zeus, she got a big kick out of appearing to mortals disguised as a mortal herself.

"I'll bet you're looking for the royal palace, stranger," Athena the maiden said to Odysseus.

Odysseus nodded.

"Follow me," the maiden said. "I'm headed there myself. But don't speak to anyone as you go," she warned, "for strangers are not welcome on this island."

Odysseus nodded again and followed the maiden toward the city. As he went, a cloud-like mist surrounded him and he disappeared from view. I smiled. Athena had learned that trick from Aphrodite, who'd hidden Paris in a cloud whenever he was about to get killed in the Trojan War.

The maiden and the mist arrived at the palace gates.

"Thank you, maiden," Odysseus said, but he said it to no one, for the maiden had vanished.

The mist remained around Odysseus as he strode into the palace and made his way to the Great Room. I was right behind him. Suddenly, Athena appeared not far from me. She looked around. I could see her, but I figured she'd chanted a spell so that mortals couldn't. Some immortals have this power to make themselves invisible. Not me, though, so it's a good thing I have my trusty Helmet.

"Hades?" she whispered. "Where are you?"

I moved closer to her. "Next to you," I answered.

Together, we watched the cloud-covered Odysseus make his way over to the queen. As he knelt down at her feet, Athena lifted the mist.

"Ye gods!" cried Queen Arete when a stranger suddenly appeared at her feet.

"Your highness," Odysseus said, "I am a wanderer washed onto your shores by the sea."

"Whoa!" said the queen, staring at Odysseus.

"You look very kind, Queen Arete," Odysseus went on. "Very kind and very, very beautiful. How about giving me a ship so I can sail back to my homeland?"

"Well, maybe, if . . . if you tell us your name and . . . something about yourself . . ." the queen stammered. She was really flustered.

"My dear Arete!" exclaimed the king. "Zeus decrees that we must never ask a stranger's name! He will tell us when he's ready. Now we must give him food and wine."

"Oh, you're right, my king," said the queen, recovering herself. "What was I thinking? Sit at our table, stranger," she added, "and we shall serve you a fine feast."

Odysseus was only too happy to sit on a golden chair and have servers bring him bread, meat, fruit, and wine. After they had eaten and rested for a while, the king turned to Odysseus.

"Now tell us," he said, "are you an immortal god come to test how we treat strangers?"

Hearing that, Athena elbowed me. We both knew that Odysseus might well pretend to be a god and see what that got him.

But to our relief, he said, "No, I am a mortal man. After wandering for way too long, I wish only to see the shores of home once more."

"How came you to be dressed in a robe made from cloth woven by my own hands, stranger?" asked the queen.

Odysseus told the king and queen how the princess's serving maids had spied him looking like a wild man and had run screaming to the princess, who was unafraid. He told how he had bathed in the river, and how the princess's maids had left him food and water.

"Your daughter's maids also brought me this robe, my queen," he said.

"I only wish my daughter had showed you to our city right away," said the king.

Odysseus smiled. "I don't think you'd have liked it much if your daughter had dragged home a sun-baked, salt-caked wild man," he said, still not giving his name.

"You may be right," said the king. "But now that we know you, and you know us, why don't you stay in Phaeacia and marry Princess Nausicca?"

"Well . . . I . . . uh . . . um," mumbled Odysseus.

The king stood up. "It's time for us to sleep now," he said. "Think about it, stranger!"

Chapter XI
THE PHAEACIANS

As you know, mortal readers, I always have my shaker of ambro-salts in my K.H.R.O.T.U. wallet. And while hanging with Athena, I discovered that she always carries a little flask of nectar in her helmet. So the next morning, the two of us were ready to turn a Phaeacian breakfast into an immortal feast.

We made our way invisibly into the royal dining hall. Athena's gray eyes lit up when she saw the spread on the buffet table. It looked scrumptious! I couldn't wait to try the Huevos

Phaeacios. We made our way through the line and as we picked up our plates and utensils, they vanished, too. Unseen, we sat down to eat at an empty two-top next to the royal family.

"How did you sleep, stranger?" King Alcinous asked as Odysseus joined the royals at their table.

"Very well," said Odysseus. "It's been a long time since I went to sleep with a full tummy."

"And have you thought about staying with us and marrying Princess Nausicaa?" the king asked.

"Daddy, stop!" cried the princess, her face turning red.

"I wish I could," said Odysseus.

"This is so embarrassing," muttered the princess.

"But I have a wife and son in Ithaca," Odysseus went on, "and I long to go home to them."

"Ah," said the king. "How old is your son? Perhaps he will sail our way one day and marry our princess."

Princess Nausicaa rolled her eyes.

"You never know what may happen," said Odysseus, and that was the truth.

The king ordered his men to ready a ship to sail Odysseus back to Ithaca.

I smiled invisibly. The Phaeacians were skilled seamen. Odysseus was as good as home!

Next, the king clapped for his bard. The bard strummed his lyre and began singing a song about the great Greek heroes of the Trojan War. He sang of Agamemnon and Menelaus, of Achilles and Hector, and of Odysseus.

As he listened, Odysseus grew sad. I knew he must be thinking of all of his comrades who'd been slain in the war, and of all his men who'd been lost at sea. At last he pushed his plate away and put his head down on his arms.

The king looked at him anxiously as the bard sang on. Athena and I ignored the singing and ate our fill. All the good things we'd heard about the eats in Phaeacia were turning out to be deliciously true. When the song ended, Odysseus lifted his head.

"Come, stranger," said the king. "Now we

shall play some games and dance and cheer you up."

Odysseus followed the king outside to a field.

"Let's go see what happens," whispered Athena. When she wasn't guarding her temple, waging war, or seeking revenge, Athena could be a fun goddess. Who knew?

Athena and I slipped outside, where young Phaeacian men were taking turns holding a heavy metal disc in one hand, spinning around, and throwing it. The idea was to see who could throw it the farthest.

One of the king's sons approached Odysseus. "Come join us in our game, wanderer," he said.

But Odysseus shook his head. "My heart is too heavy for games right now."

A young man standing nearby laughed. "I'll bet you're a trader who fell off your ship, and not an athlete at all," he said.

"Yalus!" cried the king's son. "Do not speak so to the stranger!"

Odysseus glared at Yalus, and I saw the gleam come back into his eye.

"I was an athlete once," said Odysseus. "Maybe I still am." He picked up the biggest, heaviest disc. Holding it firmly in hand, he began to spin. He spun faster and faster and let the disc fly.

The Phaeacians gasped as the disc soared over all the markers for discs that had been thrown that day. It landed far ahead of the others.

Odysseus turned to Yalus. "You wanna wrestle?" he said.

"N-n-n-no, thanks," stammered Yalus, backing away.

Down, Odysseus! I thought.

Athena shook her head. "If he shows off too much," she whispered, "the king might take back the offer of a ship to sail him home."

"Come, stranger!" the king was saying. "Watch how we dance here in Phaeacia!"

The dancers formed a circle. As the bard sang, they began to throw a silvery ball back and forth. Dancers leaped up to catch the ball and leaped again as they threw it, all with amazing speed and grace. Odysseus smiled as he watched.

"What a fine show!" he exclaimed when the music stopped. "I've seen just about everything in this wide world, but never anything like your dance."

The king seemed pleased. "My people!" he called out. "Go to your homes and find gifts for this stranger, who has not yet told us his name."

He eyed the stranger, clearly hoping that he'd reveal who he was.

But Odysseus only smiled.

"Let us give him the best that Phaeacia has to offer," the king went on at last, "so he can take it home to show everyone in Ithaca."

"All right!" cried Odysseus.

Later that afternoon, the Phaeacians lined up to give Odysseus their gifts. They held casks of wine and chests overflowing with bronze coins and gold. Seeing so much loot, Odysseus's eyes nearly popped out of his head.

The king started things off by presenting Odysseus with a large golden cup. The queen gave him a fine purple tunic that she had woven herself.

Everyone gave him something. The last man to approach him with a gift was Yalus. "Please accept this from me," he said, handing Odysseus a sword with a carved ivory handle.

"What a fine sword!" exclaimed Odysseus, taking the gift.

"I hope it will help you forgive my rash words," Yalus said. "May the gods bring you safely home."

The king's men carried all the gifts down the hill and stowed them in the ship. "After supper tonight, stranger," the king said, "my sailors will take you home."

"I should get home myself," I whispered to Athena. I'd been gone so long I hated to think how Cerbie would turn up his noses at me when I finally got back to Villa Pluto. "But I'm sticking around until I see Odysseus step onto the shore of Ithaca."

We watched as the Phaeacian servants began laying out another magnificent feast. "Definitely sticking around," I muttered.

* * *

During supper that night, the king's bard strummed his lute and sang a song about cunning Odysseus and the Trojan Horse.

Oh, the Trojans built a city surrounded by a wall,
Then came the Greeks who tried to make it fall!
That wall they'd pound and pound,
But that wall would not come down!
So the Trojan War went on and on and on.

Odysseus, a warrior with hair of flaming red,
He spoke up and this is what he said:
"I know what to do, of course,
We must build a giant horse!
That is how we Greeks will win the Trojan War!"

So they built a wooden horsey as hollow as a cave
Inside they hid twelve heroes, bold and brave!
Then they left the horse outside,
In their ships they took a ride!
All the night that horsey stood outside of Troy.

In the morning came the Trojans
And they saw the mighty steed.
"A sign from the gods!" they cried,
"That the war is done indeed!"
Oh, their hearts were filled with joy
As they rolled it into Troy
With those sneaky Greeks inside the wooden horse.

Oh, the Trojans threw a party
But at last they fell asleep.
Then out from the horse
Greek heroes they did creep.
The city gates they opened wide!
The Greek army came inside!
That is how the Greeks did win the Trojan war!

The Greeks sailed back to Greece then,
They didn't take the bus.
They'd won the Trojan War,
Thanks to ODYSSEUS!
What a wily, clever man!
To have thought up such a plan!
Thanks, Odysseus, our hero with a brain!

"How do you like that song, stranger?" asked the king.

"It's excellent!" exclaimed Odysseus. "That Odysseus! He was so clever!"

"Odysseus is such a bragger!" whispered Athena.

"I'll bet he's not finished, either," I whispered back.

"Odysseus was brave, too," Odysseus went on. "He was one of the twelve heroes hiding inside the horse, you know."

"It doesn't say so in the song," said the bard.

"Maybe not," said Odysseus. "But he was there. It was really crowded and uncomfortable in that tight space. Got to smelling pretty bad, too. It took forever for those Trojans to build wheels and roll that horse into their city, and then they partied for hours."

"Stranger!" cried the king. "How can you know such things?"

"Because," said the stranger, "I am Odysseus."

The Phaeacians gasped.

"After the war, I left Troy with twelve black

ships and many hundreds of men, all bound for Ithaca," Odysseus went on. "But here I am, a stranger in your hall, without a ship, the lone survivor of my many men."

"Hold it!" said the king. "The Trojan War has been over for nearly ten years. If you really are Odysseus, tell us what's happened to you since you left Troy."

"It's a long story," said Odysseus. He grinned. "But I tell it well."

Odysseus told the Phaecians what had happened inside the Cyclops's cave. He told of the giant man-eating Laestrygonians, who smashed eleven of his ships. And of Circe, who turned his men into pigs. He told of traveling down to the Underworld to ask advice from the ghost of the blind prophet, Tiresias; of passing Charybdis's whirlpool, only to lose six fine men to Scylla. He told of stopping on the island of the sun god and how his starving men killed Helios's cattle. He told how Zeus punished them by smashing their ship with thunderbolts. And how he alone survived the shipwreck, only to be washed up on Calypso's island, where he spent seven years as her prisoner. He told how she let him go, sending steady winds to blow him to Ithaca, and how a raging storm had sunk his ship and washed him up onto the sands of Phaeacia.

I have to admit, he told a fine tale. By the time he finished, it was late.

"I thank all of you Phaeacians for your hospitality," Odysseus said. "Now I am ready to go home."

In the dark of night, Odysseus boarded the Phaeacian ship loaded with his treasures. Again he thanked King Alcinous, Queen Arete, and Princess Nausicaa for helping him.

The Phaeacian sailors laid soft rugs on the floor of their ship. Odysseus wrapped himself in his warm purple cloak and lay down on the rugs. Before the oarsmen had rowed the ship out of the harbor, Athena and I could hear Odysseus snoring.

CHAPTER XII
MOUSE

ZZZZZZZZZZZZZZZIP!

ZZZZZZZZZZZZZZZIP!

Athena and I astro-traveled together to Ithaca. We wanted to be there when the Phaeacian ship pulled into the harbor, and so we were.

In the light of dawn, we watched the sailors carry Odysseus to shore like a sleeping baby. They laid him down under a tree, piled his treasures beside him, then sailed silently out of the harbor, bound for Phaeacia.

Athena and I walked over to Odysseus.

"He's not usually such a big sleeper," I said. "You think he's sick?"

"No," said Athena. "I put a sleeping spell on him."

"The poor mortal's been traveling for ten years to get here, Athena," I said. "Wake him up!"

"I'm about to," said Athena. "But first . . ." She morphed into a young nobleman.

I groaned. Athena had been great about looking out for Odysseus, but it was weird, the way she liked to mess with his mind.

"Give the guy a break," I said.

"Trust me here, Hades," said Athena. "I don't want him rushing to his palace before we know what's what."

She had a point.

Now she caused a cloud to form around the waking hero, making it impossible for him to see the harbor or Ithaca's rugged hills.

"Huh." Odysseus grunted as he sat up. He blinked and looked around as he got to his feet.

The young nobleman, a.k.a. Athena, walked toward him.

"Greetings, noble sir!" Odysseus called. "What land is this?"

"You're in Ithaca," said the nobleman.

Odysseus frowned. "I don't remember it being so foggy."

"Where are you from, stranger?" asked the nobleman.

A crafty look came into Odysseus's eyes. "I come from Crete," he said. "That's right, Crete. The treasures you see here are spoils from the war in Troy. I traveled home to Crete with my loot, but one of the king's sons tried to steal it, so I hopped a ship and the crew dropped me off here. Nice of them to stack my treasure up beside me, wasn't it?"

The young nobleman began to laugh and instantly turned back into Athena, allowing Odysseus to see her.

"Odysseus!" she said, still laughing. "You're such a liar."

"Athena!" Odysseus's eyes widened, then he

bowed to the goddess. "I didn't want to reveal myself in case I have enemies here."

"Always thinking!" said Athena, tapping her helmet.

"Am I really in Ithaca?" Odysseus asked her.

"Take a look." Athena whisked away the cloud.

At long last Odysseus saw his beloved rocky, hilly land. He fell to his knees and kissed the ground.

"As long as you were on the sea, I was powerless to help you," Athena went on. "You've made Poseidon very angry."

"Tell me about it," muttered Odysseus.

"But now that you're on land," Athena went on, "I'll help you all I can."

It was true. Odysseus was no longer in Poseidon's territory. He was home. I'd kept my oath, more or less, and now I could pitch in and help the great hero of the Trojan War take back his rightful place as king of Ithaca.

I yanked off my helmet.

FOOP!

"I'm here for you, too, Odysseus," I said.

"Hades!" cried Odysseus. "Two gods on my side. Awright!"

"Don't get too happy, Odysseus," said Athena. "All is not well here in Ithaca."

Odysseus's eyes flashed. "Has Penelope taken a new husband?"

"No," said Athena. "But many suitors have come to woo her."

"So I heard from Tiresias," said Odysseus. "Polyphemus told Po to make trouble for me at home. I guess this is what he meant."

Athena nodded. "Let's stash your loot in that cave over there and get to work."

The three of us moved the treasure. Then, taking a cue from Polyphemus, I rolled a large stone up against the mouth of the cave so that no mortal could get inside.

"You need a new identity," said Athena. She mumbled some words and the spark vanished from Odysseus's eyes. His skin wrinkled, his thick red hair thinned and turned to gray, and his fine robe turned to rags so worn that the long, white wild-boar scar on his thigh showed through the cloth.

"What have you done?!" cried Odysseus. "I can't show up at my palace looking like this!"

"You can't show up at your palace at all," said Athena. "Not yet anyway. First we have to make a plan for how to deal with the suitors."

"A plan?" said Odysseus. "I'm good at thinking up clever plans. Give me a moment." He paced back and forth for a while, and then said, "I had a man keeping my pigs. His name was Eumaeus, but I called him Mouse. My guess is that he's been faithful to me and my family all the while I've been gone, but you never know. Why don't I go to him now, disguised as a beggar, and test him to see if he's been loyal? While I'm testing him, he will show me hospitality and feed me. That will give us time to figure out what's going on at the palace."

Athena nodded. "Good plan," she said. "But you and Hades will have to put it into action without me. I have to go get Telemachus."

"Where is my son?" cried Odysseus.

"Out looking for you." That said, Athena vanished.

Odysseus and I walked toward the pig keeper's hut. As we drew near, dogs began to bark, and I helmeted up again.

POOF!

Just in time, too, as here came the small, wiry pig keeper. I could see why Odysseus called him Mouse, for he had a large nose and curious brown eyes that seemed to dart everywhere at once.

"Down, dogs!" the pig keeper shouted. "Leave the man be! Welcome, stranger!" he added with a friendly smile as the dogs trotted off. "What brings you to Ithaca? Ah, I forgot my manners. I'll feed you first, ask questions later. Come to my hut, old man."

"Thank you," said Odysseus the beggar.

Concealed by my Helmet, I followed them to the hut and we went inside. Mouse brought out bread and wine.

"Something in the way you walk puts me in mind of my old master, the king of Ithaca,"

Mouse said. "My heart breaks for him, and for his queen, who misses him so. I spend my days now fattening up my master's pigs for the queen's suitors. Greedy men, one and all. Oh, if only my old master would return and set things right again."

Odysseus the beggar kept his head down so as not to show the anger he felt at hearing this.

"I fear for my master's son, Telemachus, who has gone to sea to search for his father," Mouse went on. "He is almost a man now, and the suitors don't like to see him coming of age. Who knows what they have in mind for the boy? He's been like a son to me these many long years. I could not bear to lose him."

"What was your master's name, my friend?" asked the beggar.

"Odysseus!" said the pig keeper. "No finer master could a man have. Ah, me, but he has been gone so long, I fear he must be dead in some foreign land and we'll never see his handsome face in Ithaca again."

"Oh, but you will!" said the beggar. "Odysseus

is coming home," he added, "handsomer than ever."

Mouse shook his head. "You're only saying what you think I wish to hear," he said. "Now, old man, tell me where you come from and what has brought you here."

"I come from Crete," the beggar Odysseus said. "My family was a wealthy one. Rich as anything, but the fates did not smile kindly on me."

Odysseus went on and on, lying about how he'd been to Egypt and sailed up the Nile. He told of fighting with the Greeks in Troy, saying how brave Odysseus had been, how mighty!

I couldn't take any more of his lies and his bragging, so I slipped outside, astro-traveled to Athens, and spent a lovely evening with Persephone.

When I *ZZZZIPPED* back the next morning, I found Athena standing outside Mouse's hut, observing the pigs. I could see her, but once again, she'd made herself invisible to mortals.

"Pigs are very smart, Hades," the goddess

of wisdom said. "Much smarter than owls. You think I should switch my totem animal to a pig?"

"Don't you sometimes walk around with your owl on your shoulder?" I asked.

"I do," Athena said.

"That would be difficult with a pig," I pointed out. "Did you find Telemachus?"

She nodded toward a young man walking down a hill, making his way toward the sty.

"Mouse!" the young man called. "Are you home, Mouse?"

The pig keeper bounded out of his hut. "Telemachus!" he cried. Tears of joy spilled down his cheeks. "The fates are kind indeed!" He hugged the young man, put an arm around him, and took him inside.

Athena and I looked in through the doorway and saw the beggar Odysseus rise, as a beggar would, offering his seat to the young man.

"Stay where you are, old man," said Telemachus.

"He's a fine boy," whispered Athena. "Very good manners."

"The beggarman is from Crete," Mouse told Telemachus as he spread a sheepskin on the floor for him to sit on. "He's down on his luck, so he's staying with me for a while."

"I should take you to the palace, old man, and show you proper hospitality," said Telemachus. "But my home is not my own these days." He turned to the pig keeper. "Will you go to the palace for me, Mouse?" he said. "Will you let my mother know that I've made it safely home? But don't tell anyone else, for I've heard whispers that the suitors are plotting against me."

Hearing this, Odysseus scowled.

"And bring back some proper clothes for the old man," added Telemachus.

"I will!" Mouse put on his sandals. "Come!" he said to Odysseus. "I will show you the way to the stream so that you can bathe. You'll want to clean up before I get back with your clothes."

Odysseus rose and went out of the hut with Mouse. The pig keeper pointed the way to the stream, then he took off for the palace.

As soon as Mouse was out of sight, Athena appeared to Odysseus. "Now is the time to tell Telemachus who you are," she said.

"Not until you get me out of these rags," said Odysseus.

Athena mumbled the right words, and the disguise fell away, revealing Odysseus dressed in his purple robe. He looked taller and handsomer than ever.

"Sweet!" said Odysseus. And he hurried back into the hut.

Unseen, Athena and I peered in through the doorway.

"Old man!" cried Telemachus when he saw Odysseus. "Are you a god to have transformed so?"

"I am no god," said Odysseus. "I am your father, come back home after many years of war and struggle."

"It cannot be!" cried Telemachus. "Surely this is some cruel trick!"

"It is the work of the goddess Athena, who helps me," said Odysseus.

It took some talking on Odysseus's part to convince his son that he was really who he said he was, but of course nobody could talk like Odysseus. Finally Telemachus threw his arms around his father and wept for joy. Odysseus wept, too.

Then the two of them sat on the sheepskins, and Odysseus told his son a quick version of the war and of his travels, all brag but all true, too. When he'd finished, he asked Telemachus to tell him about the suitors.

"For we shall fight them," Odysseus said. "And we shall defeat them!"

"But there are more than a hundred of them," said Telemachus. "And only two of us."

"Which of my men have stayed loyal to me?" asked Odysseus.

"Besides Mouse, only Philo, the cowherd," said Telemachus.

"That makes four of us who will fight," said Odysseus.

"But how can four win against so many?" asked Telemachus.

"The goddess of war, Athena, will fight on our side," said Odysseus. "As will Hades, the mighty and powerful god of the Underworld."

Oh, clever Odysseus. He must have figured out that I was listening in!

But in truth, I wouldn't fight with Odysseus. It had never felt right to me to go around killing mortals — even wicked ones. I didn't want anyone I'd slain showing up in the Underworld and wondering for all eternity, *Did Hades slay me just to add another ghost to his kingdom?* No, I wasn't going to kill any suitors, but I'd help Odysseus in other ways.

"Are the suitors armed?" Odysseus asked his son.

"Each man keeps swords and spears on the arms rack in the Great Hall," said Telemachus. "But they have no shields or armor."

Odysseus thought for a while, and then he said, "I have a plan in mind. First of all, no matter how cruel the suitors are to you, do not be drawn into a fight."

"I won't," said Telemachus.

"I will appear as a beggar again," Odysseus went on. "I will go to the palace, and day after day, I will beg my meals from the suitors. They will get used to my being there, and after a few days, they will hardly notice me. But you must keep an eye on me," he added. "And when I give you a nod, you must slip into the Great Hall and remove the weapons from the racks. Is there a safe place you can put them?"

"The storeroom," said Telemachus. "But what if the men ask where their weapons are?"

"Tell them the swords and spears were getting blackened by the smoke from the Great Hall fireplace," said Odysseus. "Add that when they are drinking wine, it is safer for weapons to be out of the way."

"I shall do as you say, Father," said Telemachus.

"Remember, tell no one who I am," said Odysseus. "No one! Not even your mother."

"Not a word," Telemachus promised. "Not a word."

Chapter XIII
THE BEGGAR

The next morning, Mouse came whistling up the path to his hut. Seeing him, Athena quickly changed Odysseus back into a beggar.

"Telemachus!" called Mouse. "Your mother is waiting to see you."

The young man hurried to the palace.

Mouse handed Odysseus the beggar the clean clothes he'd brought.

"I want to go to the palace, too," Odysseus said as he put on the clothes. "I want to sit on the beggar's bench. Surely Penelope's suitors will fill my beggar's bowl with scraps from their supper."

"Don't count on it," said Mouse. "They are a stingy lot. But if you wish to go, I'll walk with you."

When Odysseus was dressed, he and Mouse set off for the palace.

Athena and I followed invisibly behind. We hadn't gone far when a goatherd came along the path.

"Greetings, Mel!" said Mouse. "Taking your herd to graze?"

"Out of my way, you stinkin' pig keeper!" shouted the goatherd. "You, too, beggar!" He kicked at Odysseus.

A look of fury came into Odysseus's eyes, but he only clenched his fists.

"He's holding his temper," I whispered to Athena.

"That's a first," she said. "But he'll soon have his revenge."

As Mouse and Odysseus drew near the palace, Odysseus spied an old dog sleeping on a pile of rags. The fur on his muzzle had turned white with age, and the poor thing was hardly more than a sack of bones.

Odysseus stopped beside the old dog. "He must have been a fine hound once," he said, his voice filled with feeling.

At the sound of that voice, the dog opened his eyes. He looked up at Odysseus and thumped his tail.

"This is Argos, my master's dog," said Mouse. "He's been here, keeping watch for Odysseus every day since he sailed away."

Tears welled up in Odysseus's eyes. I could tell he wanted to kneel down and hold the old dog's head. But people were passing by, and he didn't want to give himself away, so he made himself walk on.

At long last, the old dog had welcomed his master back home. And now, as I watched, Argos closed his eyes and took his last breath.

"Poor faithful old dog!" I said.

"Don't get squishy on me, Hades," said Athena. "We have work to do."

Clearly, she'd never had a dog. How thankful I was that Cerbie was immortal!

I gazed down at Argos. That dog had waited

for twenty years to greet Odysseus. What a loyal hound! If only Cerbie could have met Argos, he might have learned something about waiting patiently for a master who's gone away.

I stayed with Argos for a little while, then caught up with Odysseus and Mouse as they entered the palace. Athena and I slipped in behind them.

In those days, every palace and nobleman's house had a bench just inside the door of the Great Hall where a beggar who'd fallen on hard times might take a seat. It was the duty of the well-off diners to put a small bit of their supper into the leather pouch that the beggar held so that he might have something to eat.

Mouse walked on into the Great Hall, where the suitors were feasting on roasted pork. Odysseus the beggar took a seat on the beggar's bench.

Telemachus glanced at his father. He put some pork and a piece of bread into a bowl. "Give this to the beggar for me," he told Mouse.

Mouse dumped the food into Odysseus's

beggar's pouch. "This is from Prince Telemachus," he said.

"May Zeus grant your every wish, my prince!" Odysseus called in thanks.

After he had finished the pork and bread, Odysseus rose from the bench.

He walked among the suitors in the Great Hall, and to each one he held out his beggar's pouch. A few tossed in bread crusts, but most gave him nothing.

"What a selfish crew," Athena whispered.

"Louts!" I whispered back.

"Be generous!" Telemachus called to the suitors. "For you never know when a stranger might be Zeus in disguise."

"He's no Zeus!" cried a tall suitor. He was a well-muscled man with a full head of dark hair, but his eyes were shifty and his mouth turned down at the corners, giving him a mean look.

"You've got that right, Antin!" called another suitor.

"That beggar is a pest!" cried Antin. "I don't like pests." He picked up a stool and flung it at Odysseus.

Odysseus ducked, but the stool struck him on the shoulder.

"May you drop dead before you meet your bride, Antin!" he shouted.

The other suitors laughed nervously as Odysseus the beggar stomped out of the Great Hall. But Mouse came running after him, and I was close behind.

"Wait, stranger!" he cried. "Are you hurt?"

Odysseus only shrugged.

"Queen Penelope wishes to speak with you," Mouse went on. "Come! She is waiting to hear the news you told me about her dear husband."

I watched Odysseus for any trace of feeling. How he must long to see Penelope! But his face showed nothing.

"I will not enter the palace again until the suitors have left for the night," Odysseus said, rubbing his shoulder.

Mouse hurried off to tell this to Penelope. He returned, saying that the queen agreed to meet him later that night beside the hallway fireplace.

Odysseus sat down in the doorway to wait. He

hadn't been there long, when a big-bellied man walked up to him.

"I am Irus, the palace beggar," the man said. "Be gone!"

"There's plenty of food for two," said Odysseus.

"I eat enough for two!" shouted Irus, patting his big belly. "If you want to beg here, you'll have to fight me for the right."

Hearing this, suitors rushed out of the Great Hall to egg the beggars on, chanting, "Fight! Fight! Fight!"

Odysseus held up a hand for silence. "Old and lame as I am, I will fight," he said. "But you men must swear not to help the big-bellied brute."

"Yeah, yeah!" shouted the suitors. "Just get on with the fight."

"I hope Odysseus can resist showing off," I muttered to Athena.

When she didn't answer, I turned and saw that her lips were moving as they had when she transformed Odysseus into a beggar.

I looked back at Odysseus. Whoa! Now he

had huge muscles that bulged out of his beggar's rags.

Irus took one look at his muscled-up opponent, turned, and ran for the door.

But the suitors grabbed him. "Get back there and fight!" they cried.

The beggars began circling each other, their fists up and ready.

I could almost hear Odysseus wondering, should he knock Irus out for the count? Or just daze him?

Suddenly, Irus punched Odysseus — right in the kisser.

Surprised, Odysseus hit him back. Irus dropped to the ground. The fight was over.

"The new beggar wins!" said Antin. "But he's not getting any scraps from me."

"Me neither, me neither!" cried other suitors, who'd had too much wine. They began stumbling off to town, where they stayed each night. When the last suitor was gone, Odysseus went back into the palace.

Athena and I stuck with him. I could hardly

wait to hear him tell Penelope who he really was!

Odysseus sat down on the stone ledge of the fireplace in the hallway. He caught Telemachus's eye and gave him a nod. Telemachus nodded back, and then hurried into the Great Hall. He began taking down the weapons from the racks on the walls. He made trip after trip, carrying them down to the storeroom.

When he'd finished stashing away all the suitors' weapons, he said, "Good night, old man!" And off he went to bed.

Athena and I sat invisibly near the fire. Soon, dark-haired Penelope came down the hallway, accompanied by an ancient serving maid. I saw that she had aged, as mortals do. When I'd first met Penelope, she had a sly smile and a sparkle in her eye. Now she looked sad. For twenty years, she'd been waiting for her husband to come home. Who wouldn't look sad?

Queen Penelope took a seat on a chair near the fireplace and beckoned to her maid.

"Clea," she said, "you who were my dear

husband's nursemaid and my son's as well, bring over a chair for our guest, won't you, please? Spread it with a soft sheepskin so that he can sit down and be comfortable, for I have many a question to ask him."

Clea brought the chair and covered it with a sheepskin for Odysseus.

After the beggar sat down, Penelope said to him, "It has not been easy these long years with my husband away. As you see, all the noblemen on this island come to court me. I want none of them! But still they come, asking for my hand in marriage."

"And what do you say to them?" asked Odysseus.

"When they first came to the palace, I told them I could not marry yet because my husband's father, Laertes, was very old and I had to finish weaving his burial shroud before he died," said Penelope. "All day, I sat at my loom, weaving the shroud. But at night, I ripped out what I'd woven that day, so that shroud was never finished. I kept this up for three years, hoping that Odysseus would soon be home. But one of my maids told the suitors of my trick, and that was the end of it." She sighed. "Now I simply tell them I'm not ready to marry."

"And what do your suitors say to that?" asked Odysseus.

"They say Odysseus is dead and that Ithaca needs a king," said Penelope. "I fear that soon I must choose one of them for a husband." She looked sadly into the fire. Then she gazed at Odysseus. "Tell me, stranger, who are you? Where do you come from?"

I held my godly breath. Odysseus was about to reveal himself to Penelope!

"I was born a prince on the island of Crete," Odysseus began, and there he went, lying his head off.

I wanted to shake that mortal! Why was he lying to his poor, miserable wife who'd waited faithfully all this time for him to come home?

I left Athena to listen to his lies, and I went into the Great Hall. I paced back and forth for a while, trying to calm myself down. And as I paced, Odysseus's lies began to make a certain sense.

He'd been gone nearly twenty years, which was a huge amount of time for mortals. If he'd just said, "I am Odysseus!" Penelope might have fainted. Or kicked him out of the palace for lying. In his own weird way, Odysseus was breaking the news to her gently.

Thinking of being away and of those waiting back home, an image of Cerberus popped into my brain. I'd been gone for months. I missed Cerbie! And I knew my good old three-headed pooch must be missing me.

The Fates had said I needed to think about what was wrong with my dog, that I'd figure it out. And so as I paced in the Great Hall, I tried to think, *What can I do so Cerbie won't feel lonely when I'm away?*

When I returned to the fireplace, I found Odysseus still lying it up to Penelope. He was saying how, on his way to Troy, he'd stopped in Crete to make repairs to his ships, and there he'd met the powerful hero Odysseus.

"I've never heard such rot," Athena whispered to me.

"Tell me, stranger," Penelope said, "what was my husband wearing when you met him?"

I smiled invisibly. The queen was testing this beggar to see if he told the truth!

"He wore a purple cloak," said Odysseus. "Deep purple, like the color of the sea on a cloudy day. Let me tell you, that man looked like a million drachmas in that cloak! And I remember he wore a pin at the shoulder, too. A golden pin shaped like a hunting hound."

Tears sprang to Penelope's eyes. "I gave Odysseus that purple cloak," she said. "I gave him the pin, too, to remind him of his beloved dog, Argos."

"Weep not, my queen," said Odysseus. "For I have heard it said that your husband lives and is making his way home to you. And that he hasn't lost his looks."

"Oh, how I hope what you say is true!" cried Penelope. "But after all this time, I dare not believe it. Clea!" she called. "Come! Bring a basin of warm water and wash this stranger's feet to thank him for giving me hope."

"No, no, no, no," said Odysseus. "That's not necessary."

"Oh, but it is," said Penelope as the old nursemaid appeared, holding a basin of water. "Go on, Clea."

As Clea drew near, Odysseus turned his face to the wall. She had been his nursemaid. She had raised him!

What if she recognized him? That would really complicate his plan.

"I am happy to do this for you, old man," said Clea, kneeling down beside him. "I'd like to think that someone somewhere is washing my old master's feet right now. Oh, your feet! How like my old master's they are!" She lifted one of his feet into her basin, and as she did, his robe fell aside to reveal the long white boar-tusk scar on his thigh.

"Ye gods!" cried the old nursemaid. She turned toward Penelope to cry out the good news, but Odysseus quickly grabbed her arm.

"Shhhh!" he whispered.

Now Athena's lips began to move. I glanced at Penelope. She stared into the fire, frozen in a trance.

"Say not a word," Odysseus whispered to his old nursemaid, "or you'll put me in grave danger."

Clea nodded. "Still as a stone I'll be," she said softly, and she began to wash his feet.

When she finished, she hurried off to the women's quarters, and Athena snapped Penelope out of her trance. Once more the queen sat down beside the fire.

"Unless I can think of some way out of it, I shall be forced to marry one of the suitors." Penelope sighed. "If only I were as clever as Odysseus! Then I could think of some way to be rid of these brutes."

"I have heard that Odysseus was clever," said Odysseus.

"Oh, yes," said Penelope. "Very."

"This is just a wild guess," said Odysseus the beggar, "but do you think Odysseus might

186

recommend that you hold a contest to decide which suitor will win your hand?"

"He might say that," Penelope said slowly. "But what sort of a contest would he recommend, do you think?"

"I have heard that Odysseus had a very fine bow," said Odysseus. "And I have heard that if someone lined up twelve double-headed axes in a straight row, Odysseus could shoot an arrow through all twelve rings on top of the axes."

"That's true," said Penelope. "I've seen him do it."

"Challenge the suitors to do the same," said Odysseus. "Say something like, 'The first suitor to string my lord's bow and shoot an arrow cleanly through twelve axe rings, that man shall I wed.'"

Penelope smiled. "That is *exactly* like a plan Odysseus would have thought up!" she cried. "I shall do it!"

Now Odysseus allowed himself a smile. "Have the contest tomorrow," he said. "Who knows? Maybe bold Odysseus himself will show up."

"If only he would!" said Penelope. With that,

she bid the beggar good night and went off to bed.

Odysseus picked up the sheepskin from the chair and went out to the porch. There, he lay down to sleep, but he only tossed and turned.

"No wonder he can't sleep," I whispered to Athena. "He's planning to take on a hundred and eight suitors tomorrow."

Athena muttered whatever it is she mutters, and the restless mortal quieted. He began snoring. She was a quick one with the sleeping spells!

"He isn't going to take on the suitors alone, you know," Athena added. "Telemachus will fight with him as well as Mouse and Philo. And I'll be there."

Having the goddess of war on his side improved Odysseus's odds tremendously. But with more than a hundred suitors battling against him, there was still plenty that could go horribly wrong.

Chapter XIV

THE BOW OF ODYSSEUS

The next morning at break of day, I found Odysseus folding up his sheepskin bed. He stashed it in a corner, turned, and walked out of the palace.

Where was he headed? I followed invisibly after him to find out.

Odysseus walked until he came to a deserted hilltop. He raised his hands toward the heavens. "Father Zeus!" he called. "Give me a sign that I should go forward with my plan!"

Mortal readers, right now you must be asking

yourselves, how could Odysseus call on Zeus to give him a sign? How? He had to know it was Zeus who'd zapped his ship with T-bolts, right?

Ah, mortals. You're so unpredictable.

But then, so is Zeus. No sooner had the words left Odysseus's mouth than out of the clear blue sky came a deafening boom of thunder.

"Yesssss!" Odysseus pumped his fist in the air. "Thank you for that sign, Father Zeus!" he cried. Then he practically skipped back to the palace, he was so happy. I let that fickle mortal go on ahead.

By the time I got back to the palace, servants were busy preparing for the return of the suitors. Mouse, Philo, and Mel, the ill-tempered goatherd, had brought pigs, cows, and goats for the morning feast. Meat was sizzling on the grill.

Philo approached Odysseus the beggar. "Looks as if you've had your share of bad luck, old man," the cowherd said. "But luck can turn. May your luck change this very day!"

"Thank you, cowherd," said Odysseus. "May your words reach the ears of Zeus."

Philo leaned toward the beggar. "My old master would never stand for such goings-on at his palace," he whispered. "If only he were here!"

Keeping his voice low, Odysseus replied, "The bold and brave Odysseus shall soon return. And you shall see these suitors meet their doom."

"I hear you, old man." The cowherd slapped him on the back. "If only I could help to make that happen."

I glanced over at Athena and saw her checking out the buffet tables. I headed over to her just as the suitors came pushing and shoving into the Great Hall.

"We're hungry!" they shouted. "Give us breakfast! NOW!"

They grabbed food from the tables, ripped off chunks of meat with their teeth, and tossed the bones to the floor to be fought over by the palace dogs.

I watched those dogs, growling and snapping at each other, trying to get their share. They were fighting over the food, but they seemed to be having a fine time doing it, grabbing bones on the sly, playing tug-of-war, and chasing each other around the Great Hall.

I tried to imagine my triple-headed pooch joining in the fray. He'd like the racing and the tussle, I thought. And as the palace dogs settled down to gnaw on their bones, an idea bubbled up inside my godly brain.

But this was no time to be thinking of Cerbie. Athena appeared at my side. "Such ruffians!" she whispered, with a nod toward some suitors at the end of a long table where a burping contest was underway. "I don't know how Penelope can stand having them around."

"She won't have them around much longer," I said as Odysseus entered the room and took a seat on the beggar's bench.

"Give the stranger his share of food!" Telemachus called to the suitors.

"I'll give him his share!" shouted Antin. He plucked up a roasted ox foot and threw it at Odysseus's head. Odysseus ducked, and the foot struck the wall behind him.

Telemachus clenched his fists. His eyes flashed

with anger, but he held his temper, as his father had advised.

"Telemachus!" called another suitor. "Your father's never coming back. Never! Go get your mother. Tell her that today's the day she must choose one of us to be her husband."

"Yes! Yes! Today's the day!" the suitors cried.

Telemachus turned red in the face, but he kept his cool.

Suddenly a strange restlessness started up among the suitors. Some began murmuring to themselves. Others laughed loudly, then burst into tears. Still others staggered around the Great Hall as if they'd lost their minds.

I turned toward Athena and saw her lips moving. She'd cast a spell of madness over the suitors!

"You're a worthless pup, Telemachus!" a suitor shouted.

"You'll never be a man!" called another.

"Let's grab him and sell him to a slave ship!" cried a third.

Telemachus ignored these insults.

Athena's lips stopped moving, and the suitors quieted as Penelope walked into the Great Hall holding Odysseus's enormous bow. Serving maids followed her, carrying a quiver of arrows and a box of double-bladed axes. Each axe had a gold ring at the top so that it might be hung on a hook.

"Listen to me, you suitors who pester me day in and day out," Penelope called. "Listen, you who eat my lord's cattle, his sheep, and his pigs and drink his wine. Listen, you who say I must wed one of you."

"So you must!" called a suitor.

"I shall hold a contest," Penelope went on, "to decide which one of you to wed." She held up the great bow. "This bow belonged to my lord, Odysseus!"

Seeing it, tears sprang to Mouse's eyes.

"My dear master's bow," whispered Philo.

"The first suitor to string my lord's bow and shoot an arrow cleanly through twelve axe rings, that man shall I wed," said Penelope.

She carried the great bow out to the courtyard

and everyone followed. Telemachus dug a long, straight trench in the earth. In it, he planted the handles of the great bronze axes, lining them up straight so that a well-aimed arrow might fly through all twelve rings.

When he finished, Telemachus stepped up and took the bow from Penelope. "If I can string this bow and shoot true, none of you will wed my mother!" he shouted at the suitors. "She will stay here at the palace, and you will go away."

"This isn't part of the plan," muttered Athena.

"Can't blame him, though," I said.

Telemachus tried three times to string the mighty bow. On the fourth try, it looked as if he might succeed, but he glanced at his father, who gave his head a quick shake.

"It is too much for me," said Telemachus, and he handed the bow to a suitor.

The suitor tried to string the mighty bow, but he couldn't even bend it. "Dang!" he said. "This is harder than it looks."

He handed the bow to the next suitor, who quickly gave up. One after another, the suitors tried to bend the bow. And one after another, they failed.

"This bow hasn't been used for years," said Antin. "It must have grown hard and brittle. Maybe hot grease will limber it up."

A pair of suitors heated grease over the fire and rubbed the bow with it. But still, none of the suitors could string Odysseus's bow.

"It makes me so happy to see this," whispered Athena.

"Me, too," I whispered back. "But Antin hasn't stepped up yet."

"No," said Athena. "And he looks strong."

As we spoke, I saw Mouse and Philo slip out of the palace together. Odysseus rose from the beggar's bench and left as well.

"Be right back," I told Athena.

I hurried outside and saw Odysseus the beggar catch up with the other two. I followed invisibly after them until they stopped at a clearing far enough from the palace so they couldn't be seen.

"My friends," said Odysseus the beggar, "if

Odysseus were to appear suddenly at the palace, would you fight for your king or for the suitors?"

"For our king!" both men exclaimed.

"May it come to pass!" added Philo.

"It will," said the beggar. "For I am Odysseus, come home at last."

The two men stared at the beggar.

"Do you need proof?" said Odysseus. "I don't blame you. I am disguised as a beggar, so how could you know me? But look." He pulled aside his beggar's rags to reveal the long white scar on his thigh.

"That's where the wild boar gored you!" cried Mouse. "Bled like the dickens, that wound did."

"Our king!" cried Philo, and both men bowed down to him.

"Up, quickly!" said Odysseus. "No one must see us. If we win this fight, I will give you land and build you houses near to mine. You will be like brothers to Telemachus."

"We will fight to the death for you," declared Philo.

"To the death!" said Mouse.

Clearly both men expected to die in this battle of four men against more than one hundred. And yet they were willing to fight for their king.

"Mouse," said Odysseus, "when we go back to the palace, I'm going to ask the suitors to let me try to string the bow. They'll shout in rage at the very idea of a beggar having a turn, but no matter how they yell, you must bring me the bow."

Mouse nodded.

"When you've done that," Odysseus continued, "go find Clea, my old nursemaid. Tell her to lock herself and all the women in their rooms. Have her tell the women not to come out no matter what they hear."

"I shall do as you say, master," said Mouse.

Odysseus turned to the cowherd. "Philo, I want you to lock the courtyard gate," he said. "Secure it so there can be no escape."

"Yes, my king," said Philo.

The men went back to the palace then. One at a time, they slipped into the courtyard unnoticed.

I went back, too, and looked around for

Athena. She wasn't there. I'd never understand that goddess. Why would she take off just as the action was heating up?

Now Antin rose to his feet. "That's enough for today, suitors," he said. "Tomorrow we will send a smoky sacrifice to Apollo. He'll see to it that one of us bends this bow."

I smiled. Antin wasn't going to try to bend the bow himself until he had a god on his side!

The suitors murmured their agreement.

"Servants, bring us wine!" cried Antin.

"Wine, wine!" the suitors called.

Odysseus the beggar stood up. "Lords!" he cried. "Wait!"

"Sit down, you old beggar!" cried a suitor.

"Wise Antin is right," Odysseus continued. "Tomorrow Apollo is sure to give one of you success."

The suitors tossed back their wine, paying no attention to the beggar.

"But before you put the great bow away for the night," said Odysseus, "it might amuse you to let me have a try."

"What?" cried Antin. "No filthy beggar is touching that bow! Not while I'm around."

The other suitors shouted in agreement, all of them threatening to fling the beggar from the palace.

"Lords, stop!" cried Penelope. "This stranger is our guest. You dishonor him with your words."

I looked around. Where was Athena? I was starting to drosis. What if the goddess of war didn't show up? I'd find ways to help Odysseus, but I wasn't going to slay any suitors. Without Athena, Odysseus didn't stand a chance.

"Penelope!" shouted a drunken suitor. "If the beggar strings the bow and shoots an arrow through the rings, will you marry him?"

"He would not expect that," Penelope said. "But I will reward him with a warm cloak, a sword, and a spear."

"If the beggar wins," shouted Telemachus, "I shall give him the great bow!"

Penelope looked at him sharply. "It is not yours to give," she said.

"It belonged to my father," Telemachus said.

"Who has more right to it than I do? Go to your rooms, Mother," he added. "Weave at your loom with the other women. The bow I will give as I please, for I am the powerful son of a powerful king."

Penelope's face melted into a smile. At last her son was acting like a man! She turned and hurried to her rooms.

Now came Mouse, carrying the great bow to give it to the beggar.

The suitors shouted at him angrily, "Don't you dare give it to the beggar!" They shook their fists and threatened to rip him limb from limb. The poor pig keeper trembled with fear, but he kept walking toward Odysseus the beggar.

Things were getting ugly. Where was Athena?

I pulled out my phone and punched in her number. Straight to voicemail.

I pocketed my phone, keeping my eyes on Mouse. At last he handed Odysseus the bow. Then the pig keeper turned and hurried off to the women's quarters to tell Clea to lock all the doors.

Now Philo appeared in the courtyard. He nodded to Odysseus, signaling that the courtyard gate was locked. No escape was possible.

The suitors shouted insults at the beggar as he held the great bow. For a long moment, Odysseus stared at the one hundred and eight men in the courtyard. Then he quickly strung the bow as if it were nothing.

That silenced the suitors! They stared at the beggar, wide-eyed, not believing what they'd seen.

Odysseus chose an arrow from the quiver and notched it into the bow. He drew back the bowstring, took aim, and let the arrow fly. It whizzed through all twelve bronze axe rings and stuck in the wall. The suitors' mouths fell open.

Odysseus turned toward Telemachus. "The hour has come for us to give these lords what they deserve," he said.

Telemachus stepped forward and drew a spear from behind his back.

"Ready when you are, Father," he said.

Chapter XV

RETURN OF THE KING

Odysseus notched another arrow into his mighty bow. He sent it whizzing through the air, and Antin dropped to the ground.

One down, one hundred and seven to go.

Hidden by my Helmet, I watched Odysseus shoot arrow after arrow, slaying suitor after suitor, while Telemachus took many suitors down with his spear. Mouse and Philo ran up from the storeroom, armed to the teeth, and joined the fighting. It was four against the many, and the many were dropping like flies.

Once they understood what was happening, the remaining suitors ran into the Great Hall to get their weapons. But the arms racks were empty. The suitors could only shove tables onto their sides to shield themselves from Odysseus's arrows and Telemachus's spear.

Just as things seemed hopeless for the suitors, Mel, the disloyal goatherd, ran into the Great Room, his arms piled high with swords, spears, bows, and arrows.

He'd raided the storeroom! He began passing out weapons to the suitors.

As the armed suitors fought back, the battle heated up. A spear barely missed Telemachus. An arrow whizzed by Odysseus's ear.

Things were looking rough for the good guys. And Athena? She was nowhere to be seen. What could she be doing that was more important than helping Odysseus right now?

I spotted Mel racing back to the storeroom. I wasn't going to slay any suitors, but I could stop him from getting more weapons. I sped invisibly after him.

Two minutes later, Mel was sitting on top of a wood pile, tied hand and foot. Odysseus could decide what to do with him later.

When I returned to the battle, I spied a young warrior fighting beside Mouse and Philo. He was cutting down suitors so fast it made my godly head spin. Who could he be? And then I knew — it was Athena in disguise! About time that goddess joined the combat.

The young warrior suddenly morphed into a large black bird. It spread its wings and flew up to the rafters. From this high perch, the bird cawed out spells, causing even more chaos.

Every suitor who shot an arrow missed his target. Every spear thrown by a suitor clattered to the ground. But the spears and arrows of the four never missed their marks.

Finally the four ran out of spears and arrows. Odysseus drew the ivory-handled sword that Yalus had given him in Phaeacia. He glared at the suitors. So many were still standing! And all of them were armed with spears and swords, bows and arrows.

Could Odysseus and his crew survive this battle?

Odysseus must have thought they could, for he gave a fierce battle cry and the four men charged the suitors.

His cry was joined by a terrible roar from above. Everyone looked up to see the black bird transform itself into Athena, the terrifying goddess of war! Her whole being glowed with a blinding white light. The furious goddess held up the Aegis, her great golden shield. On it was a huge 3-D likeness of a Gorgon's head.

Still roaring, Athena swept down from the rafters. While Odysseus and his men cut down suitors with their swords, the goddess of war flew at them, shaking her Aegis. The Gorgon's eyes bulged angrily. Her face contorted with rage. The golden snakes sprouting from her head writhed and hissed at the suitors. Every suitor whose heart still beat took one look at that Gorgon and dropped dead from fright. Only when all one hundred and eight suitors lay lifeless did Athena set her Aegis down.

The four stood before her, panting and gasping for breath. They'd fought for hours without stopping and were covered in blood from head to toe.

But before he'd even caught his breath, Odysseus said, "We must carry the bodies out to the courtyard."

And the four began the task.

When they had emptied the Great Hall of bodies, Mouse went to rouse the servants, and the Great Clean-Up began. As you can imagine, it was a horrible, nasty, foul, disgusting, nauseating job. But none of the loyal house servants seemed to mind scrubbing blood off the tables or washing gore off the floor. That's how happy they were to be rid of the suitors.

"Musicians! Bards!" called Odysseus, and they came to him.

"My king," said a bard, "we never wished to sing for the suitors."

"They forced us to play!" added a musician.

"I understand," said Odysseus. "Now play and sing for me. Passersby will hear music. They will think that Queen Penelope has married at last, and that there's a wedding party going on behind the palace walls. That will give us a day or two before the relatives of the dead men come here seeking vengeance."

Even after a brutal battle, Odysseus was using his head.

Next, he called for his old nursemaid, Clea. When she came to him, Odysseus smiled. "Clea," he said, "you who knew me before anyone else, go now and tell the queen that Odysseus is home. I will clean up and wait for her by the fire."

"No happier news could I bring to my lady!" Clea exclaimed, and she hurried to Penelope's rooms. Odysseus went off to bathe.

Now Athena appeared beside me. As before the battle, only I could see her. She'd lost the glow and, I'm happy to say, the Aegis.

"Nice work," I told her.

"Thanks," she said.

"But why did you wait so long?" I asked. "I was getting nervous."

Athena laughed. "You know how mortals are, Hades," she said. "They like to think they can do things all on their own. So I thought I'd see how that went for a while."

"Four against more than a hundred?" I said. "It's a good thing you didn't wait any longer."

"I know what I'm doing, Hades," said Athena. "Those suitors were a nasty bunch, deserving of their fate. Well, I suppose you're heading back to the Underworld now."

"Soon," I said. "But I'm not leaving until Penelope learns that Odysseus is home."

"Maybe I'll stay for that, too," said Athena.

"Good call," I told her. "Leaving now would be like reading a book and stopping on the second to last page."

Before long, Odysseus appeared, freshly bathed and wearing a clean robe. He sat down on a fleecy sheepskin near the fireplace to wait for his wife.

A short time later, Penelope appeared. Without a smile, she walked slowly toward the fireplace, looking suspiciously at Odysseus.

"This is how you greet me when I come home to you after all these years?" he asked her.

"It has been many years since I have seen my dear husband," said Penelope, taking a seat on the far side of the fireplace. "How do I know you are not some pretender?"

Odysseus sighed. "I am too tired to play games."

"This isn't going well," Athena whispered.

"Clea!" Odysseus called. And when she came running, he said, "I need to sleep. Make up a bed for me in the hallway."

Now the old spark returned to Penelope's eyes. "There's no need to make up a bed, Clea," she said. "Bring the marriage bed out into the hallway for him."

Odysseus smiled a sly smile.

"Ah, she's testing him," I whispered to Athena.

"What a pair," Athena said, shaking her head.

"I built the frame of our marriage bed myself," said Odysseus. "I built it from an olive tree rooted to the ground. Its living branches make the bed posts. If you wish to move that bed, Clea, you'll have to get an axe and cut down the tree."

Now Penelope broke into a smile, and I could see in her face the girl I'd met long ago at Helen and Menelaus's wedding. The girl who'd won Odysseus's heart.

"Forgive me, my dearest husband!" Penelope cried, going to him. "I was so afraid. I didn't dare believe that what I've wished for all these years had finally come to pass." She threw her arms around Odysseus.

"That's more like it," said Athena.

After the hugging and kissing, Penelope sat down close beside Odysseus and took his hand, and he began to tell her all that had befallen him since he left her to sail away to Troy.

"I know this story," I murmured to Athena.

"Me, too," she said. "I don't need to hear it again."

Unseen, we left the palace and went outside.

"Nice working with you, Athena," I told her.

"Likewise, Hades," she said. "You know, I think I'll stay in Ithaca a while longer. There could be a problem when the relatives of the suitors show up."

"Good point," I told her. "I was thinking I might hang around for a couple more days myself. I'd like to see what happens when Odysseus goes to see his old father, Laertes."

"There's a great little diner on the far side of the island," Athena said. "The roasted eggplant is amazing. And the kebabs? Out of this world."

"What are we waiting for?" I asked.

ZZZZZZZZZZZZZZZZZIP!

ZZZZZZZZZZZZZZZZZIP!

EPILOGUE

Now you know the real, true story of *The Odyssey*, mortal readers. And now you know that it wasn't "kindly Zeus" who helped Odysseus. It was Athena, with a little nudge from me, Hades.

After Odysseus moved back into his palace and took up being King of Ithaca again, I went home to the Underworld. I was one happy god, being back at my old routines.

I hadn't been home long when one morning, as I was making the rounds of my kingdom, I heard the rattle and clank of Hermes's old bus as he came tearing down the back road to the Underworld. The bus swayed dangerously on a curve, and Hermes hit the brakes. They squealed something awful as he jolted to a stop on the banks of the River Styx.

Hermes jumped from the bus. "All right, everybody out," he called. "I mean it! Stop fighting and get OUT!"

I drove my chariot onto Charon's water taxi, and he took me across the river to meet the bus.

"Is there a problem, Hermes?" I asked when I reached him.

"This is the worst load of ghosts I've ever brought down here, Hades," Hermes said. "They bickered and fought the whole trip, clobbering each other and blaming each other for who knows what."

Ghosts streamed out of the bus, one after the other. There seemed to be no end to them!

"You really packed 'em in there, Hermes," I said. "How many ghosts did you bring?"

"A hundred and eight," said Hermes as the last ghost finally floated out of the bus.

"Oh, no, it's the suitors!" I moaned.

"All yours, Hades," said Hermes. He jumped back into the bus, started it up, and drove away at breakneck speed.

It took me the better part of a week to get the unruly suitor ghosts settled in at Motel Styx. They kept demanding roasted pork and goat shanks and beefsteaks. Somehow they couldn't get it through their ghostly heads that their days of mooching off Odysseus were over.

But judging the suitors? That was a snap. Hypnos, Thanatos, and I rounded them up and took them over to the Underworld Courthouse, where King di Minos sat in his judge's robe. When the suitors came before him, he sent every one of them straight to fiery Tartarus, where red-hot lava flows and flames burn forever.

After that, I somehow let MMMCCLXII years slip by before I began writing my book about Odysseus. That's a long time, even for an immortal. And then it took me a while to tell the whole winding tale.

When I finally finished, I gave my manuscript

to Persephone and asked her to be my first reader.

"Tell me any little thing about the story that bothers you, P-phone," I said. "Don't hold back at all."

The next morning, she took my pages and went off to Elysium to sit in the apple orchard and read. While Persephone read, I hung out beside the Pool of Memory with *The Big Fat Book of Greek Myths*. I sat in one of the big wooden chairs under the poplar trees and flipped through it, trying to decide what myth to tackle next.

I'd made it most of the way through the book when I caught sight of Persephone walking toward me. She waved and smiled. I took it as a good sign. "Well?" I said, standing up as she approached. "How'd you like it?"

"It's a page-turner, Hades," said Persephone. "Really a great story!"

I grinned. "How about I take you out for a nice dinner at the Underworld Grill to thank you for being my reader?"

"Hold it, Hades," said Persephone. She sat

down in the chair next to mine. "I have more to say. Lots more!"

Lots more? That didn't sound good. I lowered myself back into my chair.

"It felt like you didn't finish the story, Hades," said Persephone.

I frowned. "I got Odysseus back home to Ithaca, didn't I?"

"Yes, but what about his old father, Laertes?" she said. "Did Odysseus ever go to see him?"

"The day after the battle with the all the suitors, Odysseus went to the farm where Laertes lived," I told her. "He chatted the old man up and waited to see if his father knew him."

"Always the tricky one," said Persephone.

"When his father didn't recognize him," I went on, "he told the old man a pack of lies, saying he was from Sicily."

"He lied to his own father?" said Persephone.

"Of course he did!" I said. "He said he'd seen bold, handsome Odysseus in Sicily only five years before. When he heard that, Laertes burst into tears, saying that if Odysseus hadn't made it home from Sicily in five years, he was surely dead."

Persephone shook her head.

"Only then did Odysseus tell his father who he was," I went on. "But the old man didn't believe him. Not until his son showed him the scar from the wild boar wound on his thigh. After that, the two hugged and cried. Then Odysseus took his father back to the palace, where they had a big lunch with Penelope and Telemachus and Mouse and Philo."

"What about the relatives of the slain suitors?" asked Persephone. "Did they ever come seeking revenge?"

"They showed up right after lunch," I said. "Athena and I were invisibly on hand, just in case. Odysseus, Telemachus, Mouse, and Philo threw on armor, and old Laertes did, too. The five of them grabbed spears and went out to meet the angry relatives."

"It sounds as if another horrible battle was about to start," said Persephone.

"It almost did," I said. "Odysseus told

the relatives that the suitors had behaved shamefully. He said they deserved what happened to them, and because of this, the families shouldn't seek revenge. But Antin's father came running at Odysseus with a spear."

Persephone gasped. "What happened?"

"Old Laertes hadn't picked up a weapon in decades," I said. "But Athena muttered a quick spell to give him the strength of a lion, and Laertes hurled a spear at Antin's father. It went right through his helmet."

"Ugh," said Persephone.

"The other relatives were ready to attack Odysseus and his crew when suddenly Athena appeared to them," I said. "And get this. The goddess of war demanded that everyone stop fighting."

"Athena said that?" said Persephone. "Are we talking about the same Athena?"

"Yep," I said. "Even she was sick of the cycle of killing and revenge and more killing. When the uncles and fathers and brothers and cousins of the suitors saw the glowing goddess of war and heard her message, they threw down their weapons and ran away."

"And that was the end of it?" said Persephone.

"Not quite," I said. "Odysseus had been all worked up for a battle, and as the relatives ran away, he gave a wild war whoop and charged after them. But as he ran, a thunderbolt landed right in his path."

"Zeus sent a T-bolt?" asked Persephone.

"He did." I nodded. "Odysseus got the message. And ever since that T-bolt stopped him in his tracks, there's been peace in Ithaca."

"So Zeus was sick of fighting, too," said Persephone.

"Zeus didn't give a fig about fighting," I said. "But he'd finally figured out that mortals at peace send him more smoky sacrifices than mortals at war." I glanced at Persephone. "Are we done here?" I asked.

"One more thing," said Persephone. "What about that land journey that the ghost of the old blind prophet Tiresias told Odysseus he'd have to take to make up with Poseidon? You know, where he's supposed walk from town to town carrying an oar on his shoulder?"

I smiled. My P-phone didn't let a thing slip by!

"Not long after the suitor's relatives ran away, Odysseus set sail for the mainland of Greece," I said. "He put an oar over his shoulder and began walking north. He wandered until he met a man who asked him what the heck he was carrying. The man had never seen the sea or a ship and thought the oar was some sort of shovel. On that spot, Odysseus dug a hole and planted the oar in the earth. Then he made a smoky sacrifice to Po, and finally he was free of the sea god's anger. And I guess I was, too. Po never said another word to me about flooding the Underworld."

"I'm glad to hear that," said Persephone.

"Odysseus went back to his palace then," I went on. "He and Penelope had many happy years together. They died peacefully when they were very old."

"Did Telemachus become king of Ithaca?" Persephone asked.

"No, after staying at home all those years

with his mother, Telemachus wanted to travel," I said. "He sailed off and ended up in Phaeacia, where some say he married Princess Nausicaa."

"I think you should put all that in the book, Hades," said Persephone, handing back my manuscript.

"I'll think about it," I said.

"So what's next?" Persephone asked.

"I can't make up my mind," I told her.

"What about Jason and the search for the Golden Fleece?" asked Persephone.

"Another long sea voyage?" I shook my head. "Not right now. My stomach can't take it."

"I've got it!" Persephone said. "Aphrodite! You know, she wasn't born in the ordinary sense. She rose out of the sea, which is pretty weird."

I shrugged.

"The muses?" said Persephone. "That would be an inspiring book. Or no, wait. Write about Zeus and all his kids!"

"That would take volumes!" I exclaimed. "Leave it to me, Phoney, honey. I'll think of something."

Just then there was a commotion in the asphodel, and Cerberus ran out of the bushes. He bounded over to me, his three tongues hanging out of his mouths. I was giving him the old triple head rub when a ghost dog raced out of the asphodel, and Cerbie sped off after him.

"Two crazy dogs," said Persephone as the pair ran in circles, yipping with happiness before they darted off to the far side of the Pool of Memory and disappeared.

"You were the one who got me thinking about bringing the first ghost dog down to the Underworld, P-phone," I said.

"I was?" she said. "You never told me that."

I nodded. "You said Cerbie was lonely when I was away. So I found him a friend, the most loyal mortal dog ever," I said. "And later, when Odysseus showed up down here to begin his afterlife in Elysium, he was overjoyed to be reunited with his old hound, Argos."

"Put that in the book, too, Hades," said Persephone. "That makes it a happy ending."

Have I mentioned that she's always right?

KING HADES'S
QUICK-AND-EASY
GUIDE TO THE MYTHS

Let's face it, mortals. When you read the Greek myths, you sometimes run into long, unpronounceable names like Polyphemus, Nausicaa, and Antiphates — names so long and complicated that just looking at them can give you a great big headache. It can get pretty confusing. But never fear! I'm here to set you straight with my quick-and-easy guide to who's who and what's what in the myths.

Aegis (EE-jis): Athena's shield

Aeolus (EE-oh-lus): King of the Winds from the Island of Aeolia (EE-oh-lee-uh)

Alcinous (al-SIN-us): King of Phaeacia (fee-AY-shuh)

ambrosia (am-BRO-zha): food that we gods eat to stay young and good-looking

Antiphates (an-tuh-FAY-teez): king of Laestrygonia (less-trih-GOH-nee-uh)

Arete (ah-REE-tee): Queen of Phaeacia

Argos (ARE-goss): Odysseus's faithful dog

Asphodel Fields (AS-fo-del): large weedy region, gloomiest place in the Underworld

Athena (uh-THEE-nuh): goddess of wisdom, weaving, and war

Calypso (ka-LIP-so): sorceress from the island of Ogygia (oh-JI-ja)

Cerberus (CER-buh-rus): my fine, three-headed pooch, guard dog of the Underworld; I call him Cerbie

Charon (CARE-un): water taxi driver; poles a ferry across the River Styx

Charybdis (ka-RIB-diss): whirlpool sea monster; daughter of Poseidon

Circe (SIR-cee): powerful sorceress from the island of Aeaea (ee-EE-a)

drosis (DROW-sis): short for theoexidrosis (thee-oh-ex-uh-DROW-sis): old Greek-speak for "violent god sweat"

Eumaeus (you-MAY-us): Odysseus's faithful pig keeper; Odysseus called him Mouse

Eurycleia (yoo-rih-KLEE-uh): Odysseus's faithful nursemaid; also known as Clea

Eurylochus (yoo-RILL-uh-cuss): Odysseus's cousin and a crewman on his ship; also known as Rylo

Elysium (eye-LIZH-ee-um): Underworld region for ghosts of the good

Furies (FYOOR-eez): winged, red-eyed, snaked-haired immortals who pursue and punish wrongdoers; around my palace, they're known as Tisi, Meg, and Alec

Hades (HEY-deez): that's me; Ruler of the Underworld; God of Wealth; wrestling fan; author

Helios (HE-lee-os): Titan sun god; kept cattle on the island of Thrinacia (thri-NAY-sha)

Hermes (HER-meez): messenger of the gods, especially Zeus

Hypnos (HIP-nos): my first lieutenant and god of sleep; shhh! he's napping

ichor (EYE-ker): god blood

immortal (ih-MOR-tul): a being who will live forever

Ino (EE-no): sea goddess

Irus (EYE-rus): beefy palace beggar

Melanthius (mel-AN-thee-us): traitorous goat keeper in Ithaca; also known as Mel

mortal (MORT-ul): a being who one day must die

Mount Olympus (oh-LIM-pes): highest mountain in Greece; home of the gods

Nausicaa (naw-SIK-ay-uh): princess of Phaeacia

nectar (NEK-tur): what we gods drink to make us look good and feel godly

Odysseus (oh-DIS-ee-uhs) Trojan War hero; King of Ithaca (ITH-uh-ka)

Penelope (puh-NELL-uh-pea) Odysseus's wife, queen of Ithaca

Persephone (per-SEF-uh-knee): goddess of spring and Queen of the Underworld; my talented wife

Philoetius (fi-LOW-tee-us): Odysseus's faithful cowherd; known here as Philo

Polyphemus (pol-ih-FEE-muss): man-eating Cyclops; son of Poseidon; blinded by Odysseus

Poseidon (po-SIGH-den): god of the seas; father of Polyphemus, Scylla, and Charybdis, among others

Scylla (SILL-uh): six-headed, cave-dwelling, man-eating sea dragon; Po's daughter

Sirens (SIGH-runs): three singing sisters who lure sailors to their death; also known here as Thea, Pia, and Aggie

Telemachus (tel-EM-uh-cuss): son of Odysseus

Tiresias (ty-REE-see-as): blind prophet of Thebes

Zeus (ZOOS): rhymes with goose, which pretty much says it all; my little brother, myth-o-maniac, cheater, Ruler of the Universe

AN EXCERPT FROM
THE BIG FAT BOOK OF GREEK MYTHS

Odysseus is best known as the hero in Homer's *The Odyssey*. According to this folklore, after fighting the Trojan War, Odysseus takes ten years to return to his kingdom of Ithaca.

After the war, Odysseus and his crew encounter a Cyclops who kills several crewmen. Odysseus blinds the Cyclops to get away. Unfortunately, Poseidon, the god of the sea, is the father of the Cyclops. Upset, he curses Odysseus to wander the sea for ten years.

Thus, Odysseus's ten-year-long sea voyage begins. First, Odysseus and the group visit Circe, a witch who turns the crewmen into pigs. After they escape, they encounter the singing sea Sirens; the deadly whirlpool, Charybdis; and the six-headed monster, Scylla.

The surviving crew lands on an island belonging to Helios, the sun god, and the men are trapped because of a storm. They have been warned many times not to harm Helio's sacred cattle, but in desperation, they slaughter the cattle for food.

They leave the island and encounter a devastating storm. The storm kills everyone on the ship except for Odysseus, who finds himself cast ashore on the nymph Calypso's island. He is held captive there for seven years until the gods take pity on him and persuade Calypso to free him.

Odysseus sets to sea only to have his boat wrecked once more by the vengeful Poseidon. He is rescued by the sea nymph, Ino, who brings him to the island of the Phaeacians, where he meets the royal family. After Odysseus reveals what he has gone through, the king and queen decide to send him on a boat back to Ithaca.

Disguised as a beggar, Odysseus shows up at his palace, where he finds that suitors pursuing his wife, Penelope, have taken over. With the help of his son, Telemachus, and his father, Laertes, Odysseus kills the suitors. The suitors' relatives come seeking revenge, but Athena, the goddess of war, steps in to restore peace to the palace.

KATE MCMULLAN is the author of the popular chapter book series Dragon Slayers' Academy, as well as the Pearl & Wagner easy readers. She and her illustrator husband, Jim McMullan, have created several award-winning picture books, including *I STINK!*, *I'M DIRTY!*, *I'M FAST!* and *I'M BRAVE!* She and the Belgian illustrator Pascal Lemetre have recently published a graphic-novel adaptation of *Pinocchio*. Kate and Jim live in Sag Harbor, New York, with two French bulldogs. Visit her at katemcmullan.com.

GLOSSARY

aficionado (uh-fish-i-ya-NAH-doh) — a person who likes and knows a lot about something

antidote (AN-ti-dote) — something that stops a poison from working

decree (di-KREE) — to give an official order

deficiency (di-FISH-uhn-see) — a lack of something that is needed

doozie (DOO-zee) — an extraordinary one of its kind

drachmas (DRAK-muhs) — ancient Greek coins

mooch (MOOCH) — to obtain something without paying for it

rendezvous (RAHN-day-voo) — an appointment to meet at a certain time or place

salvaged (SAL-vijd) — rescued property from a shipwreck or other disaster

technicalities (tek-nuh-CAL-uh-teez) — details that mean something only to a specialist

wily (WY-lee) — full of trickery and deceit

DISCUSS!

I. Odysseus was given the chance to become immortal in this story, but he refused the offer. Would you choose to become immortal if given the opportunity?

II. Do you think Hades helped Odysseus survive his journey at sea? Why or why not?

III. Why do you think Odysseus waits to reveal his identity to Penelope when he returns to the palace in Ithaca disguised as a beggar?

WRITE!

I. Do you think Odysseus deserved the punishments that resulted in him wandering the sea for ten years? Explain why or why not.

II. When the crew was stranded on the island of Thrinacia, they faced a tough decision. The men were starving, but they were forbidden to harm the sacred cattle. Write about what you would've done in this situation.

III. Imagine that you are Penelope, and you have been waiting twenty years for Odysseus to return to Ithaca. Write a chapter from her point of view when she finds out that Odysseus has returned.

MYTH-O-MANIA

READ THE ENTIRE SERIES AND LEARN THE **REAL** STORIES!

I

II

III

IV

V

VI

VII

VIII

IX

X

THE FUN DOESN'T STOP HERE!

DISCOVER MORE:

Videos & Contests!
Games & Puzzles!
Heroes & Villains!
Authors & Illustrators!

@ WWW.CAPSTONEKIDS.COM

Find cool websites and more books
like this one at WWW.FACTHOUND.COM.
Just type in Book I.D. 9781434260161
and you're ready to go!